This is a work of fiction. Names, characters, places, and incidents are products of the author's imagination or are used fictitiously and are not to be construed as real. Any resemblance to actual events, locations, organizations, or person, living or dead, is entirely coincidental.

World Castle Publishing
Pensacola, Florida

Copyright © Kathi S. Barton 2012
ISBN: 9781938961632
First Edition World Castle Publishing December 1, 2012
http://www.worldcastlepublishing.com

Licensing Notes

Cover: Karen Fuller
Photo: Shutterstock
Editor: Brieanna Robertson

D1455467

ROYCE

The Hunter Series Book 1

By

Kathi S. Barton

World Castle Publishing

CHAPTER 1

Kasey tried to think. She was so exhausted that she could only think about walking home, crawling into her bed, and closing her eyes. The noise around the locker room dimmed as she fell asleep sitting up, no longer able to keep her eyes open. It wasn't until someone jerked her arm that she turned to stare at her boss, Mike White.

"I've been calling your name for ten minutes. What the hell is wrong with you?" She jerked her arm out of his tight grasp and looked at her locker. "I need you to work another shift, Betty, and I don't care what other plans you have."

She dropped her shoes in the open locker without looking up. "My name is Kasey, not Betty. Perhaps if you'd said the correct name in the first place I could have saved you the extra nine minutes to tell you that I'm not working for you."

She cringed at his laughter. It always reminded her of a braying jackass. "I didn't ask you to work. I said you were. Just stay away from the front until all the managers are in and you'll be—"

"Look jerk-off, I've just come off a sixteen-hour shift and I can't work anymore. I'm going home." She stood up and watched as he backed up. She was at least six inches taller than him.

"You work it or I find someone that will, and I don't mean just this shift, but permanently. Do you understand? I'm the boss, you are the employee. I'll see you out front in ten minutes."

When he walked away she nearly burst into tears. This was her third sixteen-hour shift this week at this job and it was only Wednesday. In addition to this job she had two others. She reached in and pulled out her boots to pull them back onto her aching feet.

"Are you working it?" Kasey looked over at her friend Toby. "You'll have to be unarmed to work that. Even if it is illegal for you to carry past that many hours without sleep, don't let him talk you into working armed. You'll be the only one to catch hell."

"I'll go and disarm after I pull on my boots. Could you call and tell them I'm coming down? I don't want to make prissy ass wait any more than he has to."

Kasey York stood up after pulling on her boots and tried to make her uniform look better. It was difficult to do with the thing a triple X and her a medium at best. She tucked as much of the excess shirt into her too large pants and hoped her belt, which had seen better years, held up a little longer. When she had done as much as she could she walked down the hall to the armory.

"Hey there, sweetcakes. I just heard you was a'workin another shift. Are you trying to die at a young age or you wanna go for the world record of going without sleep?"

"Hi, Uncle Jay. Nah, Tweedle-stupid is making me. I have to turn my stuff in." Kasey took the clip out of her Glock and handed it to her uncle. Then with her spotter there, she took her weapon out of the holster and handed it to him. She watched as he shot the round out of the muzzle and showed her it was empty. He handed it over to the armament and her uncle winked to her as he sauntered off.

"Honey, you need to take a break. You're gonna get sick and that ain't gonna do your momma any good." Uncle Jay handed her the paper to sign her weapon in as he continued. "You come on over to the house after work and crash. Your aunt and I would love to have you."

After agreeing she would think about it, knowing she wouldn't bother, she went back up to the front of the lobby to see what her assignment was going to be. Prissy ass Mike was taping his foot and glaring at her when she got there. She was late, he told her as a greeting, and then proceeded to tell her what she was to do for the next eight hours—as if she didn't know how to do her job.

Kasey had worked for Hunter Corporation for ten years in security. She was a part-time third-shifter that had never been able to be hired on as full-time. But it mattered little in the amount of hours she worked. In the past eight years, she'd averaged about sixty-five to eighty or more hours a week consistently. The problem was, she couldn't get the benefits without the full-time status. Benefits that would do her a world of good not just for the insurance, but for the bonuses that she wasn't entitled to get quarterly, and the pay raises.

She was just finishing up her tour of the building when she noticed that Butler, the day shift desk person, waved her over. She went to him smiling. She really liked the older man.

"Oh, darling, I gotta go. My wife made some of her famous chili last night and I'm about to die here. You think you can watch things for me for a bit? I won't be but twenty minutes at best."

Kasey agreed to watch the doors. The people coming in had slowed to a trickle now that it was nearing ten o'clock so she didn't think Prissy would mind. She kept on her feet knowing that if she sat down, she'd be out.

It had been over fifty hours since she'd been to bed. She had gotten here to work her first part of this shift at two in the afternoon the day before yesterday. Kasey had worked as a bartender the night before that and helped clean the hotel rooms with her mom that morning before coming in. She was looking at the monitors when a group of men and women came in. They all badged in but the one in the middle. Kasey turned to stop him.

"Excuse me. Sir." She'd said it louder when he all but ignored her. "Sir, you didn't badge in. I'm sorry, but I'm going to have to ask you to come back and do so."

She nearly swallowed her tongue when he turned to look at her. Now here was a man to keep a woman up all night and have her not care if she was tired. She flushed at the thought, wondering where on earth that had come from. The man next to him tried to step between her and the man, but she stopped him with a hand on his forearm.

"He doesn't need to badge in. He's—"

"I don't really care who he is. He could be the Czar of Russia for all I care. But he still needs to badge in." She looked at the man who had been silent as she and the man next to him argued. "Look, the man who owns this building went to a great expense to put this thing in. It'll take you all of two seconds to simply flash your badge at it. You don't even have to dig it out of you—"

"Look…Officer York, I don't think you—"

The man had grabbed her arm and she acted out of reflex. He was turned away from her with his arm up to his shoulder blade before he could finish his sentence. She forced him to the floor before she could think that she might have overreacted.

8

"I'm sure we can work something out that doesn't involve breaking the arm of my brother, don't you think, Officer York. Jesse?" The man helped his brother up when Kasey stepped back and let him go. "Now, you were saying something about a badge. I don't believe I've ever been stopped for one before. Is this really necessary?"

She didn't like to be a bitch, but she'd read about this sort of thing happening when a gunman wanted to take out the top guy for whatever reason. She wasn't going to be the one to let the bad guy in on her watch. She didn't think this guy looked like a shooter, but she was sure that lots of people said that about their neighbors all the time when they happened to shoot up a restaurant or place of business.

"Yes, sir. Why just last year at the Christmas party, the owner was telling us what a fine job we'd been doing keeping that little machine in proper working order. He did pay for it and all and was glad that it was being put to fine use. I'd really hate to disappoint him by letting someone get by me without letting them have the opportunity to make his day." Kasey smiled, but her stance was firm. She didn't have any idea who the owner of this building was and if asked, he probably didn't have a care in the world about that stupid badge machine, but now it was a matter of making a point. A point that she'd been right and Jesse—staring at her as if she had two heads—had been wrong in thinking she was going to just let this go.

"I don't believe I have a badge, Officer York. Perhaps you could see if I do and then bring it up to me. I'm late for a board meeting and there are people waiting on me." The man smiled at her charmingly and she figured that worked for him a lot.

"I would be happy to see if you do, sir. And if you don't, it'll only take three minutes to print one up for you. This is very important, you see. The reason we have the people badge in and out is so that in the event of a fire, we have a roll call already built in to see who is in the building when they come in and out. It's for your own safety."

He stared at her for several seconds before he walked to the desk with her. She was just pulling up the badging program to search for his name when Mike came up beside her. He jerked on her arm so hard she knew he was going to leave a bruise.

"What the hell are you doing?" he snarled at her ear. "I told you to stay out of the lobby until everyone was gone."

"This man didn't have a badge. I was just seeing if he had one." She started to put in her password when Mike pulled her back again.

"Don't," the man said in a low voice.

Kasey pulled her hands off the keyboard and Mike stepped back. She looked over at the man who seemed to be willing to look up his badge information, then she looked at her boss.

"She doesn't know what—" Mike started with a stammer.

"Apparently she does. Now step back so that she can see about my badge." He turned to her with a smile that didn't reach his eyes. "What do you need to look up my name?"

Kasey wasn't stupid. She knew something more than this badge business was going on. She looked between the two men, took another step back, and put her hands up in defense. She wasn't sure what was going on, but she had a feeling that she'd opened a can of worms that was going to get her into trouble.

"Mr. White here can finish this up for you, sir. I'm supposed to be on a round right now and…well, look, there's my replacement now." Kasey had never been so happy to see someone coming toward her as she was to see Butler. But the man had other ideas.

"You started this, Officer York, and you'll finish this. What do you need to find my badge information?" She knew then that she was going to lose her job. With a sigh of resignation she stepped back to the keyboard and, with trembling fingers, she started typing.

"Your name will do. Unless you know your employee number, either will do." She looked at him when she had put in her password and could feel the heat of Mike's anger rolling off him and onto her. "If it's not in here, we can print one in no time and you can be on your way."

He smiled again. "Of course. But let me spell it for you. Don't want it wrong on the thing, do I? My first name is Royce." She typed it in as he spelled it. "My last name is Hunter."

Her fingers stilled on the keys. Well, of course he is. *Why not?* her mind screamed at her. Why wouldn't she stop the owner of the building and make a scene about badging in? She watched as the name Hunter popped up on the screen in front of her. Jesse was there, as was another man named Daniel and yet another named Curtis. She was so fucked. But she knew that she had to finish this.

"No sir, there doesn't seem to be a badge for you. If you'd like to go with Mr. White here, he can get your picture taken and—"

"You'll do it, Officer York. I wouldn't want anyone else at this point." He handed his briefcase to his brother and told him to go on up. He'd be up shortly before he turned back to her. "Shall we?"

"I can't."

He raised a well-shaped brow at her.

"I mean, I don't have the clearance to make badges. Mr. White will need to take it from here." She moved back only to be stopped by his next command.

"You'll come along then. You should really learn all aspects of this job, don't you think?"

Yeah, she thought, it was going to do her a lot of good to know how to print a badge at the Hunter building while she was unemployed. She nodded and followed Mike. She wanted to burst into tears, but she'd learned a long time ago that tears got you nothing but a runny nose and a headache.

Mr. Hunter sat for his picture. Kasey thought she'd ask for a copy so that the next time she wanted to stop the owner of a company for a trivial thing, she'd pull out this man's picture to remind herself of what not to do. She just wanted this over with and if the daggers that Mike was sending her were any indication, she'd be done here before the ink dried on the stupid badge.

But the badge printer wasn't working for him. No matter how many times Mike tried to get it to work, it kept telling him he was putting the wrong information in. Kasey just watched him struggle.

Working nights gave her a lot of time to read and Kasey would read anything and everything. One night in a desperate attempt to stay awake when a murder mystery she'd already figured out didn't help she'd read the manual on the badge making process, including the manual on the equipment. But she didn't move forward to show Mike he was doing wrong. She just clenched and unclenched her fists until he gave up. He turned to Mr. Hunter.

"I can give you a temporary badge until the repair guy gets here later. Then when he's fixed it, I'll be able to print your badge, now that I have the picture, and bring it up to you to your office."

Mr. Hunter was staring at her. She knew that he had figured out she could fix the machine, but for whatever reason he let it go. She was more grateful than she ever thought she'd been.

"All right. But have Officer York bring it up." She looked up at him sharply when he said that. "I'll be in meetings all day, but she can catch me between them." He walked away without a backward glance.

Kasey looked over at Mike when the door to his office closed with a snap. She started to turn to leave, but he snarled at her. Before she could think about what he was doing, she was on the floor and her head felt as if it had exploded.

CHAPTER 2

Royce was sitting in his meeting with the department heads two hours later when Jesse opened the doors with a crash. Royce stood immediately and when Daniel came in too, Royce started for the door. Something had happened to their mother.

"Where is she?" he asked them as they headed to the elevator. His heart was pounding in his chest and he hoped to Christ that she was all right. "What happened?"

"She was in the bathroom when I left her. She's beat up pretty bad. Christ." Daniel leaned back against the wall as the elevator started down. "I didn't go and check on her sooner so I didn't get in there on time."

Royce nearly dropped to the floor. "Someone…someone beat up Mom? What…she's gone?"

Daniel straightened up and looked at him. "What are you talking about? I'm talking about that girl from this morning. She was beat up. Though I don't know why anyone would tangle with her, but he did."

The girl from… "The York girl? Someone beat her up? What happened?"

The elevator slid open onto the lobby. The place was quiet and the only people who looked out of place were them.

The ambulance rolled to a stop in front of the building before he could ask again what had happened. Jesse led them to the back part of the first floor where the security offices were. Royce stepped into the room just as the medics began working on...a man? He looked at his brother.

"I thought you said *she* was beat up. I'm reasonably sure you know the difference between a male and female." Royce looked back at the man from this morning as he whimpered on the floor. "Where is she if he looks like this? And where is the person who beat them up?"

Royce thought it a reasonable question. He was confused when Jesse starting laughing and Daniel flushed. Before he could ask again Mike White began howling like someone was trying to murder him.

"Quiet," Royce snapped. The room did just that. "Now, who did this to you?"

"She did. She's nothing but a fucking cunt. I didn't do...you have no idea what it's like to come to work every day afraid of your employees. She hit me. Hit me with a...she used a club. Yes, a club. I'm suing her for...oh, I'm in so much pain."

Royce looked at his brother with a raised brow.

"Bathroom. She was bleeding pretty well before I left. I told her to sit still, but she had to throw up."

Rubbing his fingers over his forehead, Royce went to the bathroom that Jesse had indicated. Royce knocked and waited. When he didn't get an answer, he knocked harder and announced he was coming in.

The room was empty. He could see where someone, presumably the girl, had rinsed blood from somewhere in one of the sinks, but there was no one in here. He looked under the three stall doors before opening them and still, no girl. He came out of the bathroom and entered the men's room just in case. No one was there either. He went to speak to Daniel and Jesse.

"She's gone. Where could she have gone? Do we know if she had someone take her to the hospital?" Royce noticed that the officer that had been with her this morning was trying to move away. "Stop right there."

"She left," he said as soon as Royce was in front of him. "She probably went home, but she ain't here. Poor girl. She won't go to the hospital, so she'll either be at her aunt's by now or her own place, though that ain't much of a place I'd want to be in if'n I was hurt."

Royce didn't know what that meant and was frankly too pissed to care. He took a deep breath and tried for patience. He had very little under normal circumstances and this was proving to push him very close to the end of his tether.

"Can you give me the address to both places? And have my car brought around." Royce turned to Daniel. "Go with White and make sure he keeps his mouth shut until we can figure this out. Jesse, can you—"

"Her uncle needs to be told. He'll wanna go with you if'n you go to his house."

Royce turned to the guard who spoke behind him.

"Her uncle is Jay York. He's the armament."

Royce heard his brother move away. He hoped to get the girl's uncle. Royce pulled out his cell phone as he stepped from the desk. He watched as the medics took a now quiet White out of the building with Daniel right next to him. The phone was answered on the second ring.

"Yes, sir."

He smiled at the voice at the other end. The unflappable Mrs. Bobbie Noel had been his secretary for nearly as long as he'd been working.

"I need some information on one of the security guards. Address, phone number, if she's been in trouble before. Her last name is York."

"Kasey York?"

That shocked him. Both that she knew who the girl was and the tone of her voice.

"What's happened? Her uncle? Or...oh God, not her mother, is it?"

"No, she's apparently hurt and I'm trying to get to her to see how badly. I didn't find out about it until just a few minutes ago." He was suddenly very tired. "Her uncle works here. Do you know how long she's worked for me?"

"Ten years." She rattled off the address. Jesse was coming toward him with an older man who he assumed was the uncle. "Bobbie, I'll let you know what I find out. Her uncle is coming now."

His car pulled up out front just as he shook the man's hand. They were headed out to the car when he realized that he had a meeting in progress. He thought about having one of his brothers go up and fix it, but decided maybe, if he didn't return, they'd go back to their jobs. Probably not, but who knew?

~~~

Kasey didn't think she was going to make it home. But when the big, ugly building came into view she nearly wept with joy. She hurt in places she'd only read about and some she didn't even know a body could hurt in. She made it up the three flights of stairs barely and had to work to get her keys out of her pocket. When she managed to get them free she couldn't make her fingers wrap around them to get the key into the lock at first, but finally got it to stick. She got the door open and was falling inside before she remembered to take the keys from the lock.

Fuck it, she thought, as she stumbled toward the bed. If someone wanted to murder her, she'd welcome them to. She didn't even care if they took their time. It wasn't like they could make her suffer any more. But she turned to take them out anyway. She wasn't really that stupid.

She cried out when she laid down. She didn't know what she'd done, but something sharp was poking at her side and she was almost afraid to look. She had just closed her eyes when she heard someone pounding at the door.

"Go away," she whispered, all that she could manage. "Please." This time, when she closed her eyes, she knew she was slipping away in a void that she was sure she should be worried about. But by then it was too late.

When she opened her eyes again her uncle was there and he looked worried. She tried to assure him she was fine, but her body refused to cooperate. She closed her eyes again.

The room was bright, which threw her off. There were no windows in her apartment and she knew for a fact that she wasn't in her room at her uncle's place. She tried to roll over, but she felt weighed down and heavy. It took her several tries to get her eyes to pry open and then a bit more to make them focus. But it mattered little because she still had no idea where she was.

"Christ, girl, it's about time. You scared me plum to death." Her uncle came into her line of sight, but he was out of focus for a few seconds.

"Where?" she croaked. It was the best she could do with the towel stuffed down her throat and the elephant on her chest.

"St. Luke's. You've been here 'bout four days. Best we can tell, you got the record for being out. You done your family name proud."

She wanted to smile, but it was just too exhausting. She heard her mom, but couldn't keep her eyes open long enough to see her.

"Mom?" She heard some shifting then suddenly her mom was there. Tears formed, but she couldn't tell if they fell or not.

"I'm here, baby. You're going to be all right now. You rest and get better. Jay and I will be here with you."

Kasey had a moment to wonder why her mom and uncle where in the bedroom with her, but she fuzzed out again. She was just drifting off when she remembered something, but it was there and gone so quickly she let it go. Besides, it hurt too much to try to chase it.

She knew that she drifted in and out a lot. She also knew that there were changes when she'd been out, that she noticed, but didn't remark on. There were things she thought she'd imagined, others she knew she had.

Like the man, Mr. Hunter. He'd been in her bedroom too. That was just plain silly. What on earth would he even care...unless he was there to fire her? Maybe, she thought, but couldn't remember why. Then she opened her eyes one day and knew she was in the hospital.

"Hello, Miss. York. I'm Abby, your nurse. Can I get you anything? If you're in pain, I can give you something for that as well."

Kasey tried to move, but it hurt too much so she looked around the room as well as she could just using her eyes and not turning her head. This place changed with every eye opening, she thought, as she took in the sofa and the big television. She looked back at Abby for answers.

"Where...where am I?" She almost dreaded the answer. If she was where she thought she was, she was in big trouble.

"St. Luke's Hospital on Main. You need anything?"

Yes, answers, she thought, but didn't ask her. "I need AMA papers now." She wasn't sure how she expected to leave against medical advice, but she had to get out of here now.

"I don't think... You won't be able to leave, Miss York. You're still hurt pretty badly."

Well, no shit, Kasey said to herself. She lifted her arm and blinked several times at the bruises and cuts on her arm. It took a full five seconds to remember what had happened and who had done this. She groaned when she remembered every detail. She looked over at the nurse who was still staring at her.

"Papers. Now. I don't have any insurance and I certainly can't afford this being unemployed." That got her moving. Abby was out the door like a shot.

Kasey was still trying to figure out how to get the bed in an upright position when her door opened again. She turned to ask the nurse how to do it when she saw who was there.

"You were going somewhere, Officer York? I'm reasonably sure you shouldn't be moving about so much just yet. The doctor said he'd have to restrain you if you tore open your stitches again. He sounded pretty pissy the last time you did it."

Mr. Hunter looked like he thought the idea of the doctor being pissy was funny. She turned away from him to work at the bed again. She felt it was better to ignore him rather than try to make her tongue work around speaking to him. When the bed moved, she cried out in pain. Maybe she should just try and move on her own.

"Are you all right?" He pressed something and she was moving again. When she cried out a second time he stopped moving the bed. For what seemed like hours but was probably only a few seconds, she heard the door open again. She prayed he'd gone away to get a gun to shoot her and put her out of her misery.

"Miss York needs something for pain. I'm afraid she injured herself trying to roll over."

The very timid "yes sir" had the door opening sound again.

"I'm going to move your bed to the down position slowly. If you need me to stop, say so."

"Stop," she told him before the bed moved. His laughter made her want to cry. He just had to be enjoying this after what she'd done about the badge.

"I'm not mad about the badge, Miss York. In fact, I'm quite impressed. No one had the guts to do what you did and it should have been done...well, years ago. I wasn't aware that the thing had been installed. Well, that's not true. I knew it had, but I didn't think of it past the installation."

"Stupid." And she was, too. She wasn't sure why he was here, but knew it wasn't good. Then she realized he'd answered her thought. "How did you know?"

"You just said...ah, didn't know you were speaking out loud. I'd like to claim that I can read minds, but I can't. I just listen very well. Here you go, the nurse has you something for pain."

"You're going to feel something warm, Miss York, then you'll feel better." Abby was standing on one side of her bed and the hunky Mr. Hunter on the other. Kasey looked up at him to see if she'd spoken out loud again and felt better when she didn't see that he'd heard her. The warmth of the medicine poured over her like liquid sex. Mr. Hunter's laughter made her think she might have spoken out loud again, but she was feeling too good to care.

CHAPTER 3

Royce was sitting at his desk two hours later. He'd probably get more work done if he'd stop thinking about the pretty little officer, but he couldn't seem to shake the image of her lying on her bed covered in blood. It had been just over a week and the image was just as clear as if it had just happened.

When her uncle and he had pulled up in front of the huge, sprawling house Royce had thought he'd had the wrong address. When Jay had gotten out of the car and walked up the steps, he looked around. The place was a dump and he'd bet his last dollar that a murder happened near here at least daily. The place didn't improve once they'd walked inside either.

Jay walked up to a couple of kids hanging out on the stairs and spoke to them. He came back a minute later and started up the stairs. Royce was surprised that the man was taking them two and three at a time, but followed him close. The boys came with them.

"They said she came in about twenty minutes ago. Said they didn't see her, but they heard her going up. She was crying."

Royce nodded.

The boy in the back went back down the flight of stairs and ran back up them seconds later. He looked over at Royce. He wasn't sure what was going to happen, but he was pretty sure that whatever it was could potentially get them all in trouble. The kid dropped to his knees in front of a door and pulled open a little black bag.

"He's gonna pick the lock," Kasey's uncle told him. "I told him we thought Kasey was hurt and he said he thought someone was, there was blood all over the stairs when he'd gone up to his apartment just after she'd gotten in."

Royce didn't ask why they didn't knock and see if she could come to the door, he just kept his mouth shut. The other kids seemed to know what he was thinking because one of them answered Royce's unvoiced question.

"Reasonable cause like them police shows. We heard her moaning, didn't you? 'Sides, she ain't gonna open the door anyway for anyone on accounta she don't supposed to be here this time a day. She's hurtin' to miss work."

Before Royce could comment one way or the other the kid at the door swung it open. When he stepped back Royce saw Jay give him some money, but couldn't see how much. Royce stepped over the threshold, thinking to ask so he could pay the man back, but the room, the bed, and the girl took his entire attention.

Her face was swollen beyond anything he'd ever seen. The eye that was turned up was closed shut and blood seeped from it. The side of her head where she lay against the bed was soaking blood into the mattress and a small stain now saturated the blanket. Her arm lay at an odd angle and her left pant leg was tight around her thigh and made Royce think if they cut the seams, the flesh would spill out. The fingers to her hand were all bloodied as well as swollen. He thought some of them might have been broken, but couldn't be sure with all that blood. He startled out of his shock when Jay shook him.

"Call an ambulance, I said. She's got to get to the hospital."

Royce pulled out his cell again and dialed the number. He'd had to ask for directions twice and assured the dispatcher that he'd remain there with her until the police arrived. Royce thought that the emergency vehicles might get called to this address a lot if they knew to ask if it was Sebastian or Jesus who had over dosed again.

"No, an injury. Miss York, Kasey York. It looks like she has a head injury, leg, and her arm. I'm betting by the way she's laying there are probably a good many ribs broken as well."

Within an hour after leaving his building, Royce was racing after the ambulance with a police escort and Kasey's uncle sitting beside him. And her injuries were more extensive than they had thought.

Five broken ribs on her left side and three on her right, a concussion, and seven stitches in the back of her head. There was the contusion to her forehead and another to just below her ear. Two of her fingers were broken on her left hand and one on her right. Her leg was sprained and there were about three dozen cuts on her body that would heal quickly; the others would take their time. The tape they'd pulled of the incident showed that when White had hit her with his fist the first time, she'd fallen back but had not been too seriously injured from what they could see. She'd gotten right up and beat the living shit out of the man until he'd gotten the upper hand by using a ball bat on her ribs. When she'd gone down he'd stood over her and beat on her several times before his brother had come into the room and wrestled the bat away from him.

White was currently in jail pending charges filed by Royce and the company. They were also waiting for Miss York to wake up enough to tell them she was pressing charges as well. Royce was still smiling when his mom walked in.

"Must be a pretty girl for you to look like that this early in the morning. Is it that Strouse girl?" She sat in the chair across from his desk. "Or is it that girl...what was her name? The one that laughed like she was a bad muffler? You remember her."

"Porsche Strouse and the muffler girl... You mean Candace Sheppard? Christ, no. She has been with more men than the NFL has players. Whoever she marries is going to need to put in a revolving door to his house. No, I was thinking about the merger deal we're finalizing tomorrow morning. You still planning to be here?"

He knew she didn't believe him by the smile. He didn't care so long as she didn't point it out.

She smiled that mom smile and leaned back in the chair. "Keep your little secrets. I'll find out sooner or later. And yes, I'm going to be here. I've been helping with this deal for three months and I can't wait to see the look on Charles' face when he realizes what we plan to do with that building. He'll be furious."

Charles Benton had messed with the wrong person when he'd pissed off Royce's mom. Annamarie Hunter was a person who got results. She'd been doing some volunteer work at the hospital when a young girl had been brought in. Jessica had been fourteen, pregnant, and beaten. She lost the child and then died two days later, but not before telling the police who had beaten her and why. Her daddy had said no child of his was going to shame him.

Of course nothing could be proven. The man who'd beaten poor Jess had been killed only days later and everything pointed to him acting on his own. But nearly everyone knew better. Charles had made no bones about the fact that he cared very little for his daughter and less about the child she'd lost.

"We have everything in place to start the reconstruction of the building on Monday. Then all the players are lined up to make it so that we can reopen as 'Jessica's House' the month after. It's amazing how many people have agreed to give their free time to work with this house."

Royce leaned back in his chair and regarded his mom. "You're an amazing woman. How come I never realized that before?"

She snorted at him. "You knew. You're too much like your other brothers to say so unless you need something. What is it now? A girl you've knocked up? Someone who won't sleep with you and you want me to tell her what a great catch you are?"

"Mother," he said with mock shame. "The things you think of me. And I know better than to try and have unprotected sex. You've told us often enough growing up what would happen if you found out. I, for one, want to keep all my appendages, thank you very much."

She flushed slightly and Royce grinned. "I love you, son. But you do know that you irritate me to no end, correct?"

Laughing, he got up and grabbed his jacket. "Come on, beautiful. Lets you and I have lunch together. I want to run a few things by you."

They were to the lobby when his cell phone went off. He pulled it out to see that it was from the hospital. Royce answered with a bit of concern.

27

"Mr. Hunter, it's Abby from the hospital. Miss York is...she's... Oh my, there is someone in the room with her and they are going at it loudly, sir. You told me to call when there—"

"I'm on my way. If whoever it is tries to leave before I get there, try to at least get their name. I should be there in about five minutes." Royce turned to his mom. "I'm sorry, but we'll have to do this some other time. I have to—"

"I'm going with you. And don't even try to argue because you know it'll do you little to no good and only make you later. Let's go."

Sighing heavily, knowing she was correct, he nodded and went to the doors to his car. The limo was just coming to a smooth stop as they stepped out into the warm sunshine.

~~~

"I said to get out of here. I don't give a shit how you found out, just get the hell out of here." Kasey pulled the pillow out from behind her head and threw it at the man in front of her. "Get out!"

"Now, Kasey, that ain't no way to treat your daddy. I've been busy, is all. You know how it is trying to make a living. I was just wondering about how you're gonna sue that fancy company you work for is all."

Gilbert MacDonald had run out on them when Kasey was born. He'd been pissy, Kasey's mom had told her, when he'd found out she was pregnant and ripping mad when Kasey had been born a girl and not a boy. Over the years he'd come around when he wanted something, money usually, and to knock around Leah York, Kasey's mom. Until Kasey got big enough to fight him back, then he would only come for money. Like now.

"I don't have any idea what you're talking about. I got hurt and I have no insurance and no money and, if you go near my mother, I'll hunt you down and hurt you so bad you'll feel it for a month."

Gilbert moved closer to the bed, his eyes dark with anger. She'd forgotten that she was helpless and that was the way he liked his women. When he drew back his fist to hit her she closed her eyes and waited for the pain. She couldn't fight him in the condition she was in.

"You'll back away from that girl right this minute or, so help me, I'll be causing the pain." Kasey turned to see what the hell Mr. Hunter was doing here. "Are you all right?"

She nodded. Mr. Hunter had her father in a full nelson. She wasn't sure how that had happened, but was immensely glad that he did. Kasey started to explain who the man was, but a woman, a very beautiful older woman, came to the other side of the bed and started checking her injuries.

"She doesn't appear to be hurt, Royce. Why don't you take the trash out and I'll make sure the nurse comes in and gives her something for—"

"You know, I'm right here. I don't need anyone to bring me anything for pain, and I certainly don't need you to call her if I did." Kasey looked at the woman. "You have to be related to him. I've never met a pushier bunch of people in my life."

Kasey wouldn't admit how badly she hurt right now. Nor would she admit how grateful she was for the intervention of Mr. Hunter. The woman simply started laughing, much to the surprise of Kasey.

"Oh my, you have to be the secret. Yes, I'm related to Royce. I'm his mother, Annamarie. And you would be…"

"Mother, don't do this. She works for me and was—" He'd just stepped back in from taking her father out of the room. She didn't worry about her father coming back soon, but he would be back.

"I *worked* for you, not *work* for you. I was fired. Remember? And I haven't the slightest clue what sort of secret you think I might be. And frankly, I don't care. I have to get out of here." Kasey looked over at Royce when he growled. "Oh grow up, you big jerk. Not everyone has money dripping from their fingers."

Mrs. Hunter started laughing even harder at that. "You're not the least bit intimidated by him, are you? Good. A woman shouldn't be afraid of their mate, I think. What happened that landed you—" She looked over at her son. "The officer from the lobby?"

"Yes, I'm...I was Officer York. And now I'd like for you both to be going now. I've got plans to make and places to go." Kasey wasn't sure how she planned to execute anything, but she had made them. She raised a brow at them both when they pulled up chairs.

"Now, tell me who that man was and why he has reason to want to hit you. I must admit, I've been under the same strain since I've met you, but not enough to actually follow through." Kasey glared at him as he continued. "You have been a pain in my ass since you stopped me in the hall of my own building."

"Then don't make rules you have no intentions of following." She laid her head back on the bed and closed her eyes. "Haven't you heard that 'he who makes the rules is a man of great leadership?' I don't think I've ever read where 'I make the rules and I say fuck them.'"

She'd forgotten about his mother and looked over at her when she laughed. The woman was certainly his mother. She had the same glint in her eyes when she was laughing. Kasey looked over at Royce. His glint didn't seem to be from laughing.

"Miss York, are you in the habit of biting the hand that feeds you? And I'll decide when you are fired from my company. Who was that man and what did he want with you?"

She turned away from him to answer. She wasn't ashamed of being a bastard child, but she was ashamed of the bastard who was her father. "His name is Gilbert MacDonald and he's my father. At least in the sense that he was the sperm donor that created me. He's not been much of anything else. He and my mother never married." Kasey looked at the door when it opened.

"Miss York, your lunch is here. Shall I bring it in or wait until later? You know what the doctor said." Abby seemed a bit miffed again, but Kasey didn't care.

"I know what he said and I still don't care. Bring it in please, but don't expect me to eat any more of it than I did this morning. I've told you three times I don't care for it. And I want to go home."

Even to her ears she sounded childish, but no one would listen to her. She didn't want any broth and she certainly didn't want any hot tea, all they would give her. She turned her head away when the tray of "food" was put on the little table.

"What is wrong with you? Are you nasty to everyone or just those that try and help you? Christ, I don't think I've ever met anyone as caustic as you are." Royce stood up and started taking lids off of the containers. "You'll eat every bit of this or, so help me, I'll hold you down and pour it down your throat."

Kasey glared at him. "Try it." Her voice was low and full of intent. He paused for several seconds as they glared at each other. She was glad that she'd made him think. She wasn't

31

one of his minions who jumped when he barked. And she didn't fucking work for him.

"Royce, why don't you go get you and me a nice sandwich from the deli across the street? I'm sure that Miss York and I can get this lunch business squared away." Neither of them looked at Annamarie. "Royce."

He finally looked at his mother and gave her a short nod before leaving. He turned to look back at Kasey before he walked out the door and that look said volumes. He told her that if she hurt his mom, she'd be a dead woman. Well, she had news for him, she didn't care.

"Oh goodness, no wonder you don't want this. It's crap." The woman began taking the rest of the lids off the other bowls and cups as she tisked around. "Good heavens, is this suppose to be helpful or kill you? This won't do, not at all. Why, if I had a dog…nasty."

The nurse came in a minute later and with instructions to take "this vile tray away." The nurse left. Annamarie pulled out her cell phone.

"Darling, pick up some of that wonderful chicken broth while you're there and see if Dominic has any of that delicious beef broth he uses for his roast beef sandwiches…yes, I did look at it and it's nasty. Hold on, let me ask her. Kasey, sweetheart, Royce wants to know if you would care for some tea with your lunch or would you like some bottled water?"

Kasey was reasonably sure that it hadn't been put that way, but didn't quibble over the delivery of the question. She told her that she liked iced tea, not hot, and water would be fine if it wasn't available.

CHAPTER 4

"She has worked for you just over ten years. But for reasons I can't figure out, she's only considered part-time."

Royce looked at his brother Jesse. "What do you mean? You know we have a number of employees that are considered part-time. It works out well for all of us."

"Yeah, but for her...look at her average weekly pay. I checked with records and the girl averages about eighty hours a week. I mean, Christ, that's more than you work in a week and she does it consistently."

Royce picked up her payroll sheet. It looked like over the past year she'd worked enough hours to triple her income. He looked over at her hourly wage and then back at Jesse.

"She ever apply for a full-time position?" He knew the answer before his brother showed him the applications. There were over three dozen of them.

"She's been applying for a full-time spot since she was hired. Those are only over the past three years. She can't apply and be turned down but every six months." Jesse pulled out another sheet from the file in his hand and handed it to him. "These are her job performances. In order to be eligible for the yearly bonus, it's required that you score a seventy-five or above. The bigger your score, the bigger your bonus."

Her scores were fantastic. Nothing below a ninety-seven and several one hundreds. All the comments seemed to center around her good deeds and her ability to do her job. He looked at Jesse again, knowing he was missing something.

"She can't get them. The bonuses. She's not eligible because of her part-time status. White had been keeping her as part-time so that his bonus would be bigger. The less he gives out, the bigger his is for his department. Kasey was caught where he wanted her. A great employee who needed to work and who did it very well and no bonus."

Royce leaned back in his chair and read the comments in the spaces for the supervisor she worked for. *"Exemplary work." "Good work ethic and code of conduct." "Amazing trainer, keeps things running when I'm not available."* And there were more than that.

"Find out what her bonuses would have been, change her status to full-time retro from the day she was hired, and give her the benefits that she's entitled to." Royce took the next sheet of paper he handed him. "Christ, you're good."

On this sheet were the bonuses she'd been entitled to, a check for the amount, and the change in her status. Both needed his signature to complete. Also, there was a form to have her promoted to White's position.

"I thought you'd want someone in the position that you knew would do a good job. She's the best you have in that department. From all accounts she runs the department when he's not there or even when he was. There's not one employee there who wouldn't jump for her."

Royce figured as much. Every time he saw one of the other officers, they asked about her. She was very well liked. He wondered if anyone of them had felt the bite of her tongue when she was pissed, but didn't ask. She was entirely too mouthy as far as he was concerned.

"Let me think on this promotion for a bit. She won't be back for awhile yet so I have time." Jesse laughed and Royce glared at him. "She isn't exactly what I'd consider management material is all."

"Sure. And this has nothing to do with the fact that you're attracted to her, I suppose. Mom said she isn't afraid of you. I think that's hilarious."

But Royce had stopped listening. "Attracted to her? When hell freezes over. The girl has the most annoying, mouthy, bitchy...well, as far as I'm concerned, there aren't enough adjectives to describe what she is. Attracted to her. Mom, right? She put you up to this. Well, she's wrong."

Jesse stood up and gathered his papers. "Me thinks thou doth protest a bit too much, brother dear. Admit it, she's gotten under your skin. Even I can see that."

"Under my skin like a festering splinter. Get out of my office before I have to call in the security that you're so fond of."

Jesse left laughing. Royce wanted to get up and pound his brother in the head until he stopped, but knew that it would only make matters worse. He leaned back in his chair to wonder why his mother thought he was attracted to Kasey.

She was beautiful. Her hair was the color of fall, dark and light reds and browns that made him think of warm nights in front of the fire snuggled under a blanket together. She'd probably hog all the blankets, but it would be fun trying to take them from her. Or trapping her beneath them to grab a few kisses. He stopped that train of thought.

Her eyes were a shade of gray he'd never seen on a woman before. Steel gray with highlights of dark blue that darkened when she was pissed. He'd seen them that color more often than not and he smiled. He did seem to push her buttons.

KATHI S. BARTON

She was tall and, with her ill-fitting clothes, he'd been
hard pressed to figure out if she was as big as she looked or
just sloppy. He'd heard from her uncle that she'd been
requesting new uniforms for over three years and every time
they came in, they were bigger than before until she just
stopped trying. Jay thought it was White trying to put her in
her place. Royce was beginning to see that he might have
been correct. Then he wondered if Jay knew what his niece
had been putting up with and decided that he hadn't. Jay York
would have torn the man to pieces for his niece.

He'd been intrigued by her the moment she'd stopped
him in the lobby. He'd never been stopped before and, while
that surprised him, he'd wished her timing had been a bit
better. But when White had come up and started ordering her
around he wanted to see how she'd react to finding out who
he was. He supposed that he wanted her to see him as
godlike, the man of all men. But she'd only seemed like she
was going to the guillotine.

She'd handled that well enough, better than he'd
expected. She'd not backed down nor done anything but her
job. He smiled. She was a pain in his ass and though he
wouldn't admit it to his family, he was beginning to be
attracted to her. He picked up his coat and the check and
started for the door. Time to pay the piper, he thought, and
see her face when he gave her the check.

~~~

Leah watched the man coming toward her. She knew who
he was. Her daughter had complained about him endlessly for
the past few hours. And she had described him to the letter.
All the way from the way he walked like he owned the
ground beneath his feet to the top of his dark curly hair that
needed a good comb through and a pair of scissors. Leah
smiled when she saw the frown on his face. Here was a man

36

who could give her daughter more than she ever dreamed. If either of them were to stop bickering at each other long enough to see it.

"She's getting a bath. Well, they're trying to give her a bath. She's hurting so bad that they had to give her a shot to ease the pain, but she wants to be clean more," she told him when he stood next to her. "She claimed that she couldn't stand her own odor."

Royce looked at the door and then back at her. "She can be quite vocal when she's displeased, can't she? Would you like to go get a cup of coffee while we wait? I've not had lunch yet either if you're interested."

Leah nodded. "Thank you. They just started so they may be awhile. She asked me to leave so that she could cuss without repercussions. I think I might have heard a few of them before I got the door closed. That poor nurse."

"Yes, well your daughter can be nice when it suits her. Not to me, but I've seen it a time or two with you." Royce smiled and took a bit of the sting out of his words. "I'm sorry. You probably don't want to hear me bashing your daughter right now."

Leah laughed. "Kasey always has been a bit headstrong. I think I wanted her to be independent so badly I over-encouraged her to be outspoken as well." They were seated in the large cafeteria when she spoke. "She's my biggest champion. I love her with all my heart."

Royce laughed. "She does love you too."

They ate for a few minutes before Leah looked up at the man again. "I'm dying. Soon, as a matter of fact. I have an inoperable brain tumor that is slowing killing me. Or quickly, I suppose. I have less than six weeks left on the year they gave me. I don't think it's...I won't live to see her married or happy with a family of her own."

He looked embarrassed then he looked her in the face. "My secretary told me about your illness. Bobbie, I think she knows your brother Jay. She said you'd been ill for a while before they found it."

"Yes. Kasey blames herself for that, but I can't convince her that it's not her fault. She seems to think if she'd not gone away to school and had been home to see what was happening, I might have been able to get it taken care of. But she couldn't have. It was too big before anyone found it. I'm just lucky that I've had the past few years to prepare and be with her." Leah looked away, her heart suddenly too full to think.

"I'm sorry, Miss Y—"

She smiled back at him when he started to apologize to her. "I didn't tell you for your sympathy, Mr. Hunter. I told you because I wanted you to know about my daughter. She's not as bad as she seems...well, not near as bad. She just hates hospitals. I do, as well. When I was first diagnosed she spent nearly all the time with me. Six months, as a matter of fact. And the hospital hadn't been...they weren't kind to me as they are with her right now. The administration frowns on people without insurance coming to take up their bed space when others with money can be there. Kasey works too hard to pay the bills I incurred. And she refuses to let me help her when I can work. She seems to think it's her duty to take care of me."

"She is owed some money from my firm. A great deal of money. If I give it to her, what will she do with it?"

Leah smiled at his question. She thought the man knew what her daughter would do with the money, but she answered anyway. "She'll pay what she can on my bills. If there is any left over, she'll insist on paying this one as well. Kasey hates to owe anyone anything."

Royce straightened up, clearly offended. Leah wondered if the two of them realized just how much they were alike. Both had a pride that rolled off them in rivers.

"She was hurt on the job and I take care of my employees, Miss York. She will have to learn to live with disappointment if she thinks I'm going to let her pay on my bills. And if she tells you any differently, you let me know. I'll set her straight."

Leah threw back her head and laughed. "Oh, Mr. Hunter, you are in for a big surprise if you think anything I say to her will make a difference when she has something set in her mind. Kasey is the most stubborn woman I know and she will tell you that all on her own." Leah laughed again. "I love my daughter, Mr. Hunter, very much. I love her more than a mother loves her daughter. Without her...without her, I'd have died a long time ago. But she said I can't. And for whatever reason, I haven't."

He nodded with a soft smile. "Call me Royce. And for as much as I hate to admit it, I admire her stubbornness, but that doesn't mean I'm going to let her get by with it."

"Call me Leah, and you have my fondest hopes that you can *try* and get through to her. As I have said, she is extremely stubborn." To herself, Leah thought, *and my biggest hope is that I get to see you two come together.*

They went back up to her room twenty minutes later. Kasey was alone in the room when they entered and glared at Royce when he came into the room with her. Leah hid her smile and sat in the chair next to the bed without commenting on her looks at Royce.

"Do you feel better, honey? Your cheeks are red. Are you in pain?" Leah had to bite her cheek to keep from laughing when Kasey turned as best she could away from the man on the other side of her bed.

"No, I'm not taking any more pain crap. All it does is make me sleepy and I can't do anything while I'm asleep."

"That's the plan, you know," Royce said. "When you're asleep, you can't hurt yourself and your body has a chance to rest. It's called cause and effect. You should try and practice that a bit more. You might learn something. Take the damn drugs and get better."

The only reaction Kasey had was to stiffen, but she didn't answer him. Instead, she continued to look at Leah. Kasey smiled tightly. "I've been making arrangements with Uncle Jay. He said that I could move in with him as soon as I can get there. Aunt Suzy will be thrilled. And he said that he'd hook up the Internet if I still needed him to. It'll help me—"

"You are not going anywhere until I say so," Royce cut her off. "I know for a fact that the doctor said you'd be here for another week or more until you could even begin to think about moving about. And if—"

Kasey turned on him immediately. "Listen to me speak, you overbearing, pigheaded asshole. *I* do not work for you. *You* are not my boss. I don't even know…what are you doing here? Get out. Shoo."

"No." Royce turned to look at Leah. She could see the strain on his face and, for whatever reason, she thought it was the funniest thing she'd ever seen. "Could you give us a few minutes? I'd like a few words with your daughter."

"You're not tossing my mother out. I want you to get out. I don't even like you. You are the most stubborn, egoistical dickweed that —"

Leah didn't know what she expected, but she certainly didn't expect him to lean down and kiss Kasey. Smack her, yes, maybe even flip her over and beat her bottom, but not kiss her. Leah stood up and left the room when she heard her daughter moan. There were some things a mother just didn't want to know.

Out in the hall Leah leaned against the wall and waited for the elevator, smiling. She knew then that Kasey had met her match and couldn't be happier for either of them. She just hoped that she'd be around to... A slight dizziness came over her and she had to hold on to the railing before she fell. But it left as suddenly as it had come over her. Weakly, she moved toward the elevator and stepped inside of the opening.

Time was running out. She knew this as well as she knew that she her daughter was going to be as happy as she ever hoped for her to be. Leah pushed the button to take her to the ground floor and held onto the railing again. Soon, too soon, she'd be gone and she was happy that her little girl would have someone to hold her when this was over. Leah knew her daughter wouldn't be happy with her if she knew what she was thinking, but there were some things a mother *did* want to know. And Leah wanted to know that her only child would have someone to care for her, to hold her when she was no longer able to do it.

KATHI S. BARTON

CHAPTER 5

Royce pulled back from her mouth regretfully. He couldn't help but take another taste before he stood back. Then he nearly took another taste when she moaned again. Christ, the woman tasted like sex and heat all rolled into one. He watched her expression change from dreamy to pissed in a few seconds. Damn, she was amazing, and he found himself wanting to see her going from pissed to dreamy this time. He watched her face and knew the exact moment when she was herself again.

"What do you think you're doing? You can't just kiss me like that. I told you before to get out of here and don't come back."

He grinned at her. "You behave or I won't kiss you again. Now, we have some things to discuss. It's about your position in my company." Her sputtering nearly had him laugh, but he wasn't that stupid.

"Kiss me ag—are you insane? You most certainly will not be kissing me again. And for the hundredth time, I don't work for you. I was fired before that idiot hit me and even if I hadn't signed off on it, I still wouldn't work for you." She pulled the covers up over her shoulder and glared at him. "You're nuts."

"Most likely. But that doesn't mean that you didn't enjoy it. You kissed me back, Miss York. And did a damned fine job of it too. I liked the way your tongue swept over mine. The way your warm breath tickled my cheek when you moaned. Damned if I don't want to taste you again." As he leaned in to take another nibble, she pushed her hand against his chest.

"Don't you dare."

Royce felt his cock harden. Her voice, low and hot, made the skin on his body seem to come alive and his blood to run like hot lava through his veins. He couldn't have stopped now if his life depended on it. "Kiss me, Kasey," he whispered to her. "Kiss me again and let me feel your need. Please, baby." He ran his tongue along her lower lip before he ran it along the seam of her lips. "Let me in, love. You know you want to."

When she opened under his teasing, he touched his lips to hers. Soft and firm, warm and cool. He was amazed at how many different sensations a person could feel from a kiss. But he should have known she was giving in too easily. He barely escaped from her mouth before she bit down at his tongue. As it was, he got a nip on his lip.

"Damn it, woman, that hurt. You could have just said no." He stepped back when she reached for his groin. Somehow, he knew if she got him there, he'd be lucky if he'd be able to piss much less father children.

"I told you no. I've been telling you no for a week. What do you need, visual aids? Just leave me alone."

He heard the small sob in her voice and nearly stepped to her again, but her look stopped him. She pulled the blanket over her head this time and he had no choice but to leave. He needed to think anyway. Things were going much too fast, even for him. "I'll be back later. I have something for you and neither of us is in the mood to discuss it right now. I'll be...I'll bring my brother back. That way if you try to have your way with me again, I'll have someone there to save me."

He had no idea why he'd made that parting shot, but he got a laugh out of her growling at him. Had something bigger than a pillow been close, he was sure she'd have thrown that at him instead.

Royce left her room and walked to the elevator. She affected him like no other woman had and he wasn't sure he liked it. He really didn't dislike it because she did bring out feelings in him he'd never had before. He really wasn't sure he liked himself, either, for trying to make her do things she didn't want. He had the limo take him to work and then he had a meeting he had to go to later. One that he hoped would take his mind off the beauty in the hospital. He was sitting at the long conference table when his mother, his brother Curtis, and Charles came into the room.

Curtis was the company lawyer and Daniel was their personal one. Having two lawyers in the family gave them everything they needed and then some. Jesse had become the law enforcement part of the company, including any Internet security problems they might encounter. Also the laws governing trade that way. And Royce supposed people would say he was the money maker, though all of them were wealthy. Royce had learned at his mother's feet how to buy and sell not only on the market, but also in businesses. Royce, the oldest, had taken over the company when their mom semi-retired five years ago. And he'd been making money since.

Curtis gave them all a copy of the paperwork on the newest acquisition that Hunter Corporation was taking on and settled back to explain any and everything that the paperwork entailed. He was a very detailed person and Royce knew without reading the sheets in front of him that everything would be covered and they'd have every loophole buried so deep that it would take another fantastic lawyer like him to find it.

"We purchased the Benton Works for one point three million dollars and your back taxes will be paid with a portion of the proceeds," Curtis said to Charles. "As soon as we are made aware that the taxes have been paid, we'll take possession immediately and shut it down. After thirty days the building will reopen and any and all employees of the aforementioned building will be rehired at that time. You, Benton, will pay their unemployment wages until that time."

"Tell me again why I'm paying their wages? I could care less how they make their money. I won't own the fucking building any more. Why should I care where they work?" Charles really was a self righteous bastard most of the time.

"Because," Curtis said with a bite to his voice, "it's part of the deal. And frankly, Benton, I could care less if you make a thin dime off this sale, but you will do it as we've lain out or the IRS steps in and takes everything else you have."

"You should have been a lot nicer to the people you used on your way up the ladder, Charles, and maybe a few of them would have helped you out on your way down." Annamarie smiled as she spoke to him. When Charles stood up both he and Curtis stepped in front of him. "See, my sons love and respect me. You have nothing. And at the rate you're going, you never will."

"So this is revenge? This whole thing has been about Jessica? My God, woman, she was knocked up. What the hell was I supposed to do, support her and her bastard kids?"

"Yes. It's called being a parent. Sign the papers, Charles, before I go after a few more of your businesses."

Charles snatched up the paper and signed where each tab had been marked. Then he did the same for the other two copies. One would be filed in the courthouse, another would go to the files in the Hunter Corporation, and the final copy would be held until Charles paid his taxes. Once he's signed off Curtis nodded to his mother.

Royce braced himself for the explosion. This was the part where their mother announced what the Benton building was going to be used for. It was the only reason they'd purchased the building, to rub his nose in what he'd done.

"The Jessica Home for Unwed Mothers thanks you, Charles. I'm going to make sure that each woman that comes through our doors knows the reason why we're here and why it's named after your daughter." Anger boiled off the man the moment their mother finished speaking.

"You fucking bitch. This has been because I wouldn't let my daughter have a bastard child?" When Charles stood this time, so did Annamarie. "I'll get you for this. See that I don't."

"I'm not sure how much *getting* you'll think you can do from prison, Charles. Last I heard, the IRS is going to seize all your properties." His mother smiled at Benton before she sat back down. "Why, I was able to purchase your home on Wilson for a song. Seems when you make a reasonable offer, the government doesn't mind a few taxes being not paid."

Before he could make another step toward her the door opened and three men from the security team walked in to escort him out. When the door closed behind them Royce looked over at his mom. "You really bought his house? I hear that's a really beautiful home. Congratulations. "

"Yes, it is pretty. It's your wedding present if you ever get married. You're the only one still living in an apartment and I thought you could use it. Curtis helped me get it when things started to turn sour for Charles. Poor man, but he made his bed, now he must lie in it." She sat back in her chair and looked him straight in the eye. "Got any prospects in mind?"

Royce frowned when the first name that popped in his head was Kasey. He'd not known the girl all that long and had only kissed her once…well, twice if you counted when she'd tried to take his tongue off with her teeth. But to his mom he simply answered no. "I don't think I ever want to tie myself down. It's hard enough to be single. I can't imagine what it would be like married with a woman dragging you down all the time." Royce stood before she could comment. "I have to get some work done if we're going to have dinner this weekend. Thanks for the house, Mom. I love you for it."

He was sitting in his office an hour later with the same report in front of him. He didn't know what he'd been thinking of, but he knew it wasn't work. Royce looked up when Jesse walked in after a hard knock.

"You know that girl…Officer York, that was hurt the other week?" he asked as a greeting. Royce nodded, almost afraid to know what she'd done now. "Did you know she has a degree in Business Management?"

Royce didn't, but only shook his head. "Every person who gets out of college now days has some kind of Business degree. What of it?"

"Not a Bachelors, but a Masters degree. And she has another in Law Enforcement. Her minor both times has been another language. One is Spanish and the other is Chinese. She's a smart cookie."

Royce was shocked. He didn't think Kasey was stupid, but to have two Masters Degrees as young as she was couldn't have been easy. Royce wondered aloud why she worked for them as a security guard and wasn't running some corporation.

"Don't know. Her file didn't say. But I will tell you this, as soon as she gets up and about, I'm going to ask her out." Jesse stood to leave. "She's a cutie and Mom likes her."

Royce didn't move. He wanted to go after his brother and tell him...tell him what? Leave her alone? Enjoy dating her? Royce didn't like either thought. He didn't want to date her and he didn't want his brother to either. He grabbed up his coat to go and have a few words with Miss York. He didn't know what, but he was going to talk to her about something. He was halfway to the hospital when his phone rang.

"She's gone. She checked herself out of the hospital about ten minutes ago," Abby said. "I went to lunch and when I returned, she'd already done it. Did you know that you can get AMA forms off the Internet? She had them signed and gave them to the head nurse when her uncle showed up to get her."

"Son of a bitch."

~~~

Jay watched his niece very carefully. She was upset, that was for sure. But about what, he didn't know. She was talking to Suzy like she always did, but he could hear the strain in her voice.

They were coloring at the makeshift table when Suzy began to cry. "No, no, no. Suzy want red. Want red. Want red."

"All right, but you know that you can't have it until you calm down. I won't play with you if you can't behave." Kasey held the red crayon in her hand just so that Suzy could see it. "You want it, you can't act like a spoiled baby."

"Want. Suzy want." When Suzy stood up and stomped her foot, Jay started to move toward her. She wouldn't hurt Kasey under normal circumstances, but since she was hurt, it would be bad. But Kasey held her ground.

"I have it and if you want it, you know what you have to do." Suzy stood there glaring down at her niece.

Jay had been caring for his sister since their parents died nearly ten years ago. Suzy had Down's syndrome. And at fifty-one years old and nearly two hundred and fifty pounds, she was like a very big eight-year-old with the strength of a grown woman. But she loved Kasey, loved her since the day Leah had brought her home from the hospital. And Kasey had been caring for her aunt since she figured out how to.

"I like red. It's pretty like the flowers." Jay had to smile at his sister's reasoning. "You need to let Suzy color with it. Please."

There was a knock at the door before Kasey answered. But before he left the room, he saw Kasey hand the coveted crayon over to her. The laughter followed him into the front hall. Peace once again reigned. Well, for now, he thought when he saw who was on his front porch.

"Mr. Hunter. How are you tonight? I didn't..." Jay looked back behind him, sudden dawning hitting him. "She didn't tell you. She told me that you knew she was coming here."

"No, I didn't. I told her to stay there until the doctor released her. She needs proper medical care and I've come to take her back so that she can get it."

Jay nodded. Not that he was agreeing with the man, but he knew why she'd left and he almost understood it. "You telling her to do something is the same thing as telling her to do the opposite, you know. Kasey always has been stubborn like that. The sure way to get her to do something is to tell her she can't. Works nearly all the time."

Laughter from the living room had him turning. He was worried about leaving them alone so he thought to get rid of the man before Kasey figured out he was here.

"Look, Mr. Hunter, she's here now and doing fine. I can't—" A crash had him nervous. "I have to go. You see yourself out."

The scene in the living room wasn't a bad as he'd imagined. The small table that had been set up for the coloring books had been knocked over and Suzy had moved to the television. Kasey was lying back on the couch with her arm over her eyes, but she didn't appear to be hurt. Jay moved toward the mess, intending to clear it up. Royce took that moment to start into Kasey.

"What the hell do you think you're doing? I told you to stay at the hospital. Don't you listen to a damned thing anyone tells you?"

"You didn't tell me anything, you arrogant ass, you ordered. I don't take orders from you or anyone else. And what the hell are you doing here anyway? I thought you'd be thrilled not to have to bother with me anymore."

"*No.* No, no, no, no." Suzy put her hands over her ears and started rocking. "No, no, no, no, no."

"Now look what you did. You've upset my aunt. Get out." Kasey tried to move, but cried out in pain when she did. Jay dropped the books he had and started to go and help her, but Royce was there before he was. Jay watched as the man paled and seemed terrified. Interesting, he thought.

"What is it? Tell me what...are you hurting? Damn it, Kasey, you have several broken ribs. They could be back in your lungs if you don't lay still."

"Go away," Kasey whispered. "Please, you're upsetting her."

Jay moved to his sister. "Come on, Suzy, let's you and I go and make some dinner. Royce, will you stay?"

"No. I want to stay, too. Sit. I'll be good." Suzy pointed to the chair next to him and Royce looked at it.

"I'd like to sit next to Kasey for a few minutes, please. She's hurt and I want to make sure she's all right." Royce didn't raise his voice like some people did when dealing with Suzy. As if raising your voice would make her understand better.

"Royce, I'm going in the kitchen. Kasey needs her pain pills. If Suzy gets out of hand, yell. I'll come back and get her." Jay walked to the kitchen and picked up the house phone. He called Leah. "You're not going to guess who's here. Royce Hunter. He's watching over our Kasey."

"Has he hit her yet?" Leah asked with mirth. "Those two are like two sticks of dynamite ready to explode. He kissed her today, did I tell you?"

She had, but he let her tell him again. Jay leaned his head against the cabinet above the phone and listened to her. He loved his sister very much and knew he was going to miss her more than he could imagine.

"You should come over and eat with us. I have plenty. I made spaghetti and meatballs. There's a salad too."

"No, I'm sort of tired tonight. I think I'll go to bed soon. But you call me tomorrow and tell me how it went. And Jay…"

"Yes, love."

"Don't you dare say a word to him if he wants to spend the night. She's in no shape to have sex and maybe she'll sleep better if he's there."

Jay laughed. "Honey, you know as well as I do if they want to have sex, all the casts in the world aren't going to stop them. But I won't. And I'll call you tomorrow." He let the tears fall. Leah was his baby sister and he'd do anything in the world for her, but there wasn't a damned thing he could do about this. He turned to finish up dinner as he thought about the couple in the other room.

He'd worked for the Hunter Corporation since before his own Jean had died some twenty years ago. Their marriage hadn't been a great one, not even a good one, but it had been fair. Jean had never cared for Suzy and she knew it. When Suzy had had some difficult days, Jean would lock her in the closet and leave her there. It wasn't until he'd come home from work early to see it for himself that he'd forbidden her to do it again. After that, Jay had asked for help from the local church and Suzy would spend the day with some of the ladies there. She'd grown to love them.

Then Leah had gotten sick after his Jean had died in an automobile accident in icy weather all those years before. Kasey had come home and held them all together. To this day he had no idea what she'd given up to come home to help and she wouldn't tell him either. From Leah, all he'd gotten was that she was happier here.

When dinner was ready he went back into the other room. He stood in the doorway and watched Royce with Suzy. When he noticed Jay standing there he nodded over to Kasey.

"She's hurting. Do you think she can have something now?" Jay knew it was bad when she didn't argue. He handed the water and pain pills to Royce and took Suzy to the kitchen. He came in just as they were finishing up. "I'd like to stay tonight. She's asleep now, but when she wakes I want to see if I can convince her to come back to the hospital with me." Royce sat down. "Or bring her back to my house. I can hire someone to keep an eye on her. She won't be happy, but I'll know she's fine."

"You love Kasey. She's my favorite. I love her more than chocolate. You love her too."

Royce stared at Suzy, but made no comment. Jay didn't either. The man simply looked pole axed, but about what Jay couldn't say. He showed Royce where to take Kasey and let him settle her in her big bed. He just hoped they all weren't making a mistake.

CHAPTER 6

Kasey woke warm. And stiff. It took her a few seconds to realize she wasn't alone in her bed. When she put her hand on the arm around her waist, she realized it wasn't her aunt. The arm was most assuredly male.

"Do you need something else for pain?" the voice rumbled sleepily in her ear. "I'm not sure how often you can take them, but it's been about five hours."

"Mr. Hunter?" She couldn't move. She knew she should pull away from him, but she just couldn't make her body work.

"Kasey, I'm in bed with you. Don't you think you should drop the Mr. Hunter bit and call me Royce? You did earlier tonight." His breath was warm on the back of her neck. "And we have kissed."

"Why are—" Her train of thought stopped when he placed and open-mouthed kiss on the back of her neck. And then when his leg moved over her uninjured one, she moaned.

"Why am I what?" His voice seemed to melt over her. She had to try and concentrate very hard on what she'd been thinking about before he'd kissed her.

"Why are you in bed with me? Shouldn't you be home, in your own bed, away from me?" She swallowed hard. "You need to back off."

"I'm in bed with you because you're here." He kissed her again before he continued. "And there is only one bed in this room. A nice bed too. I haven't slept this well in…wow, it's been months."

"I'll give you the brand name. Get off my bed. And go home. Home is where you should be, not here." Kasey tried to roll away, but short of rolling on her sore hand and arm, there wasn't much she could do. She tried inching over and away from him, but he pulled her back.

"Lay still. You keep moving around like that and I'll begin to think you're ready for some things I've had on my mind since I felt you press your bottom against my cock." He rolled his tongue into the shell of her ear and nipped at her lobe. "Things that'll make both of us forget where we are."

Kasey closed her eyes only to see her own ideas of what they could be doing and she popped them back open. "You can't possibly want to have sex with me. I'm…I'm not your type at all. I'm a…a…stop that."

He was running his hand up and down her thigh, getting closer and closer to her panties. When his fingers stopped on her hip bone she didn't know whether she wanted him to move off or closer to her pussy. She squirmed when he didn't move.

"I want to touch you, Kasey. I want to feel how wet you are and then taste your cream off my fingers." She closed her eyes at the seduction in his voice. "I want to feel you come around my fingers and lick them dry of you. Will you let me, baby? Will you let me make you come?"

His fingers moved down her thigh and up again. This time he didn't stop at her hip, but brushed along the elastic at the top of her curls. While his fingers were running back and forth over her skin he was adjusting her around so that her head was toward his and he took her mouth.

This kiss was different than in the hospital. This one was hungry, needy, and so much more heated. As his tongue traced along her lips he slipped his finger under her panties. When his tongue brushed along hers, dueling slightly, his fingers found her clit and he slid between her folds. His moan seemed to come from his mouth and into hers and straight to her pussy, making her cream more on his hand.

"You're so wet," he growled in her ear. "Wet enough if I wanted to enter you, I'd slide deep. Do you feel what you're doing to me?" He pressed his cock into her ass. She moved gently back and heard him moan again.

"Please," she begged him.

He pulled his fingers free of her and brought them to her mouth. "Taste, baby. Taste what I'm going to when you come. Christ, I want to bury my mouth over you. Lick your pussy until you come down my throat."

When she lapped at his finger he rocked hard into her ass. She was so close to coming she knew that if he kept this up, she'd be begging for him. When he moved his fingers back to her pussy she started riding him, riding his fingers even as he rocked into her ass from behind.

"I want to be inside of you. I need to…let me, Kasey. Let me bury my cock into you. I'll be as gentle as I can."

"Yes. Please, yes. Hurry, I need…hurry, please." She was nearly sobbing when he tore her panties from her and when she felt him pull back she whimpered. Then he was there. His cock hard and hot between the cheeks of her ass.

"Lift your leg for me. Gently, don't hurt yourself." She couldn't think beyond that he was going to be inside of her.

Pain was the last thing she could think of. When she lifted her leg, wrappings and all, he entered her.

Neither of them moved for several seconds. Her body was on fire and she knew as soon as he moved, she was going to come. Now, she needed to come right now. With his hand on her hip, she moved back and felt him shudder.

"Please, Royce. I need to…please, fuck me."

He moved back then rocked forward twice as he filled her. She lifted his hand and put it over her nipple and he bit at her shoulder. The climax came quick, grabbing her hard and making her cry out. Royce moved quicker now, and his fingers of his free hand moved between her legs and he pinched her clit. Again she came, hard. Before she could catch her breath he was pushing her again.

"Come, baby. Come now, come with me." His command brought her again, and this time she felt him fill her; his cum seemed to touch every part of her body as he shuddered to release inside of her. Even before he pulled free she was drifting off, her body sated and relaxed.

When she woke later the room was still dark. She started to stretch, but a slight soreness and tightness felt like it had taken over her body. Then she remembered what she'd done…what they'd done. She knew she was alone in the bed and started to roll over when he spoke from behind her.

"Please tell me you're on the pill. Or at least some sort of birth control."

She finished rolling over before she answered. Royce was as far away from her and the bed as he could be and still be in the same room. He had even moved her chair from her desk to accomplish it. She shook her head and then realized he couldn't see her well. "No. I've never…there was never any reason to be and I couldn't afford them." He swore harshly. "I didn't plan this."

"So now I suppose you're going to claim that I forced you? I didn't. You were just as much a part of this as I was. Unprotected sex wasn't why I came here."

That got her. "Then why the fuck did you come here? I certainly didn't invite you. In fact, I told you to leave several times. As a matter of fact, why don't you just get out? That's what you want anyway."

"What about the child? What if in our stupidity we created a child? Then what? I won't marry you. I have no intentions of marrying anyone."

She couldn't believe how badly he was tearing her up on the inside. But before she'd let him know what he was doing to her, she'd die first. She turned her head away and tried to regain some control over her emotions. "If there's a child, I'm quite capable of seeing to it myself. I don't want you either." Tears fell and she knew it was seconds before she was going to break down. "I'd like for you to go away. Just go away and leave me alone."

She heard him stand up before he answered her. "You'll tell me if there's…if we…"

"Yes." It was all she could manage.

She heard him shuffle around; a shoe hit the floor and she thought he was undressing and her heart began to pound in her chest, but then he was near the door. He seemed to hesitate then he spoke again, softer this time.

"I left a check on your dresser. It's for—"

"I don't want your money. What kind of person do you think I am? You lousy fucking bastard. Ge—"

"It's your wages," he hurriedly told her. "Back wages. You should have been taken on as a full…I meant to give it to you yesterday. Before this, before we… It's the bonuses that you should have received. I hadn't…I didn't know you'd not been receiving them."

She didn't move, didn't speak. She was afraid of what she'd say, what she'd do. When she heard the door open and close softly she waited. She wanted to make sure he'd left, he was out of her life, before she gave in. When she heard the soft crunch of gravel in the drive and saw the small skim of lights go over her window, she knew he'd left her. And Kasey did something she'd not done since she'd found out about her mom's tumor; she cried. Cried so hard she heard her uncle come to her door.

~~~

Royce was sitting at the stop light a few blocks from his apartment when his phone rang. His breath caught thinking that Kasey was calling him back when he realized it was his brother. He answered with a sharp hello and a demand of why he was calling him at five in the morning.

"You asked me to meet you at the gym, asswipe. I'm so going to knock the shit out of you if you bail on me when I got up to work out with you."

"No, I'm...I'm on my way now. I had...I overslept. I'm ten minutes away." Royce closed his phone, made a right at the next street, and went to the club house. He didn't want to meet with his brother; he didn't want to meet with anyone. He wanted to go home and think about the woman's bed he'd just left and what he'd said to her.

He'd been sitting there thinking about what they'd done for over an hour before she woke up. Her soft mew when she rolled over nearly made him want to strip down and crawl back into the warm bed with her again and see what other ways they could make love and not hurt her. Even as quick and short as their first time together had been, it had been more satisfying than any other time in his life. He wasn't sure if that made him happy or pissed him off more.

They'd had unprotected sex. Great sex, but still unprotected. He'd been alternating between excited about seeing her swollen with his child to being pissed that she might be pregnant. Then he thought about the complications of being married. Not to her, just in general.

He didn't want to be married, plain and simple. Being married meant loss of freedom, not being able to just come and go as he pleased. Of course, she'd be in his bed every night. But that too was something he wasn't sure he could handle. Not that they didn't have great sex this one time, but every night? No, he didn't think...no, he knew he couldn't be faithful to just one woman. He'd done right in making sure right up front that he wasn't going to marry. And hell, she seemed all right with it too.

It did sting a little that she'd said she didn't want him. He didn't think he was all that bad of a person. He just didn't want to shackle himself down. That didn't mean that they couldn't get together sometimes and have some fun. But to say...he realized he was going about this all wrong.

They'd agreed. If there was a kid, she'd tell him. If not, then he was off the hook. He pulled up in front of the gym and turned off the engine. He knew the odds of her getting pregnant were fifty-fifty, but he didn't think the odds were going to be that good.

He just knew that she was going to be calling him up in a few weeks and demanding that he marry her. Well, that wasn't going to happen. He was going to be prepared for such an event. He pulled his bag from the truck and went inside feeling like he'd figured her out. Yes, this was going to be a piece of cake.

CHAPTER 7

Kasey knew her uncle was mad at her, but she didn't care. Well, she did, but he loved her. It had been two weeks since Royce had left her and she knew it was time for her to move out. She still had her bandages on, but she was hobbling around pretty well and she didn't have to have someone feed her at every meal.

"I still think you should wait until you get at least your arm out of the sling. It's not hurting me having you here."

Kasey took a deep breath before answering. "I can't stay here forever. I have to have my own place, my own things again."

"You could, you know," he told her softly. "You could stay here forever. I love having you here. And Suzy has been so happy since you moved in. She'll miss you."

"I'll miss her too. And I'll miss you, but Uncle Jay, I have to leave. I can't...I don't..."

"I know, baby." He hugged her to him before he finished. "I'm so sorry, honey. I wish I would have told him to go home. He shouldn't have treated you that way."

She'd told him that Royce and she had had a fight. He'd wanted her to go back to the hospital and she'd thrown him out once and for all. She'd not told them about the sex, and she'd not mentioned that while he wanted to know if they'd stupidly created a baby, he wouldn't do anything about it. But she did tell them about the check.

The check had been for nearly thirty grand. Ten years of bonuses and back wages. She'd taken the money and paid her mother's hospital bills and doctor bills and put the rest of it in her mom's account. She smiled when she thought of her mom's anger when she'd told her what she'd done with the eight thousand left over.

"You'll do no such thing. You take that money and spend it on something extravagant for yourself. You've worked far too hard to put that money to no good use in a bank."

"I'm going to get a job that I can work during the day and come home at night. I'm going to work one job, just one, and at the end of the day, be finished with it. When my vacation comes around, I'll take one, go somewhere fun, and not worry about the other three jobs I have. But best of all, I'll know that you'll be taken care of. That you'll be secure, safe, and have money to fall back on when you don't feel like going to work." Kasey held her mom's hand. "Please let me do this for you. Please. I need to know that you won't be treated as a subhuman without insurance the next time you get sick. Let me do this for you." She nodded. Kasey knew she didn't like it, but she would do it. For her, for them.

The apartment where she'd been living until just over six weeks ago was rented again. Calling it an apartment was like calling Kennedy National Airport a small stopover, but it had been hers. She was grateful to her uncle for getting her things packed up for her and putting them in the garage. She'd been looking for something suitable for several days now and thought she'd found someplace. The work she'd been doing for the college was helping make that dream a reality.

Kasey had been doing some typing when she'd had time before she'd gotten hurt. At three bucks a page to correct term papers and redo them, it had been an easy source of income. Now it took her a little longer, but the typing was helping to exercise her fingers after being broken and she had been able to put some money aside. She had almost enough to put a deposit on the place and pay some of the utilities. Her uncle was lending her the rest.

The apartment was on the ground floor of an older house. She had a bedroom, small kitchen that spilled out into the dining area, and living room. The bath was large by most standards, but it was clean. There was plenty of hot water, Mr. Rhodes told her, and she'd have a parking place right out front. He reminded her of her uncle and after a few minutes of walking around the place, she decided to take it. It would be her first real place since she'd come back home.

Three days later, she was moving in. Her uncle had asked a bunch of the guards from work to help him set her up and she had more help than she needed. But it was great seeing the gang and she sprung for pizzas and beers when everything was set up and things were put away. Her mom brought her an old kitchen table and chairs and her uncle gave her the couch from his basement. She was smiling happily when they all left. But as soon as the door closed, her face crumbled.

Nights where the hardest. She was lonely even when she'd been staying with her uncle and he would sit and talk to her after he'd come home. He never mentioned work other than to talk about one of the guys and she never asked about the one person she wanted to. Royce and his hurtful words still haunted her.

Two weeks. It had seemed forever ago when he'd told her they'd been stupid. She supposed they had been, but that didn't make it any less hurtful. She wondered if there would ever be a time when she didn't feel the ripping pain when she thought of what had been said. Crawling into her bed, she let the tears fall. She had no reason to hide them now, no reason to bury her face in the pillow to hide the hurt. But she did anyway. As she had been doing every night since that night, she cried herself to sleep.

~~~

"If you snap at me one more time I'm going to knock the shit out of you. I'm fucking sick to death of having you bite my head off every time I open my mouth."

Royce looked at Curtis and counted to ten. He knew he'd been snappy, but if one more person asked him what his problem was he was going to scream. He was fine, damn it. Fucking wonderful. "I'm not snapping at you," he said between clenched teeth. "I'm trying to make a point. If we don't get this contract signed then the rest of the projects in that area will fall apart. It's because of this one building that we can't move on the others."

"I know that. But short of going into Klingner's office and demanding that he sign off on it, there isn't a hell of a lot I can do. The man is giving up his entire business, one his father's father started. He can't just let it go without some thought."

"Then he fucking should have been a better businessman." Royce took another deep breath before continuing. "Look, I'm having a bad morning and I—"

"You've been having a lot of bad mornings and at the risk of getting my head bit off again, what the hell is wrong with you?" Curtis closed the file, apparently finished discussing it. "Does this have anything to do with that little officer?"

Why did he have to mention Kasey? It wasn't as if he didn't think of her on his own several hundred times a day. He wanted to snarl at his brother to leave it alone, but he knew that if he didn't talk to someone soon he was going to have a breakdown or one or all of his family was going to hire a hit man and take him out.

"If I tell you something, can you keep it to yourself? I mean not even tell Mom? I'm serious."

Curtis got up and opened the door to his office. Royce heard him tell Bobbie to hold his calls and not to disturb them until they said. She agreed. Royce knew he'd been snapping at her too and wondered why she hadn't poisoned his coffee yet.

"All right," he said when he sat back down. "Tell me what has you so bitchy that you'd take it out on all of us. Does it have to do with Miss York?"

"Yes." Royce got up to pace. "She and I had sex." He didn't say more because frankly, he wasn't sure how to proceed.

"And that's bad how? She's a pretty little thing. She seems to have more than the normal brain cells in her head that you normally date. And the prettiest gray eyes I've ever seen. Was the sex that good or that bad? Don't tell me you couldn't get it up around her. Oh, Royce...no wonder you're pissy."

"That's not it, you fucking asshole. I didn't use protection. And she isn't on the pill." Royce might have laughed at his brother's expression at his announcement if he'd been in the mood to find anything funny.

"When? Is she pregnant? Has she, Christ, Royce, is she demanding that you marry her? I can certainly help you out with any kind of arrangements you want to make. I would suggest a pre-nup before you marry—"

"I'm not marrying her. And I don't know if she's pregnant or not. She said she'd let me know. But I already told her I wasn't going to marry her." That sounded just as bad now as it had when he'd told Kasey. "Marrying for the sake of a kid is no way I want to go through the rest of my life. She understands that."

"I see." Royce looked at Curtis when he spoke. "Actually, no, I don't. You play you pay, buddy. Unless, of course, she tricked you. Did she? If so, I can see where you'd not want to attach yourself to her, but you know what Mom is going to say. Once she beats the shit out of you anyway. She's been preaching safe sex to us since before we knew what sex even was."

"She didn't trick me. I... Damn it, Curtis, I fucking don't want a kid. I don't want a wife, and I certainly don't like this waiting. I want to call her up and demand that she tell me. I've been making myself and everyone around me nuts and for two weeks. I can't take it anymore."

Curtis sat there for several minutes while Royce watched him. He could see his brother's wheels turning. Of all of them, Curtis was by far the most analytical when it came to problem solving. "She probably has a doctor's appointment soon from the incident here. Let me make a few calls and see if we can get a test done without her knowing it. That way you'll have your answer and she'll be none the wiser."

"Is that even legal?" Curtis shrugged. "Then don't do it. I won't have you getting into trouble over my mistake. I'll get my answer and then everything will be all right. I'll know she's not pregnant soon and then get on with my life."

"Do you really think it'll be that easy? You think she's not pregnant?"

No, Royce thought. She'd be pregnant and he'd be in court trying to fight his way out of any demands she had been dreaming up. "I don't know, but just in case, I want you to draw up some papers telling her that I'm not going to be a part of the kid's life if she stays out of mine. I'll pay her whatever is reasonable for support, but that's it."

Curtis nodded. "And Mom?"

That, Royce had no clue. "I'll cross that bridge when I come to it."

Feeling better than he had in a week, after Curtis left Royce sat down to go over some of the things he'd been putting off. By five o'clock, he'd managed to get four projects completed and two more started. He was very proud of himself. It was nearly six o'clock when he left his office and he was home by six-thirty. Home to his new house.

The house was lovely. Huge, but very well made. The furnishings had been sold; he'd not had the same tastes as Benton and was having two of the bedrooms converted into an office on the second floor. The kitchen had been remolded recently so, when he'd moved in, he'd been able to cook for himself. He was enjoying the ability to play around in the kitchen again.

The house was a three-story colonial that had been built of brick. The front of the façade had been sandblasted of the white paint some years ago and the dark color meshed well with the four large white columns that graced the front. The double doors, oak and very old, opened into a large entrance hall that opened to a long, curving staircase that led to the upper floors.

Seven bedrooms filled the second floor with five baths. The halls were knotty pine and wide with indirect lighting along the floors. The stairs leading up to the third level were also curved and oak and spilled out into a room alight with skylights everywhere. Royce had been using the room as a large office/gym until the office on the first floor was ready. He had no idea what he was going to do with the room once he moved his things out of it, but it was a really nice room.

The master suite was on the main level. There was a fireplace in the bath and in the main room. His mom had told him that the two rooms off from the suite were a nursery and a maid's room. He hadn't been in either of them since he'd moved in. Royce cringed whenever he thought of his mom hinting about using those two rooms.

The kitchen and living room, the two rooms where he spent the most time, were the most furnished. He had gotten a living room suite that he wanted, complete with overstuffed chairs and a big screen television, and the kitchen was perfect.

He was standing in front of the refrigerator when his phone rang. He frowned when he realized who it was.

"I'm not happy with you, young man."

Royce straightened up when his mother spoke.

"Why? What did you hear?" If Curtis told her what he swore he wouldn't, Royce was going to kill him.

"Why didn't you tell me that Miss York quit working for us? I think after all we've been through with her you'd at least let me know when she decided to move on."

That was news to Royce too. "I didn't know. When did she quit?"

"She told human resources this morning. I probably wouldn't have found about it then if I hadn't been in the lunch room when one of the guards happened by. He told me that she had another job and that she had moved into her own place."

Royce slammed the door closed. Damn her. She had no right to move on when he was so fucking miserable that he was barking at everyone. He realized his mom was still speaking.

"I can understand that she'd want to not be in that office again. Poor girl probably has nightmares just thinking about it. But to up and quit without letting us find her something else. Well, I have to tell you I feel slightly miffed. And you say you didn't know either? I thought the two of you had gotten close."

Closer than she thought, he wanted to tell her, but didn't. "Do you know where she moved to? I'd like to make sure it's a better place than she was in before. That place was a dump."

"No. All he told me was that he'd been to her house just over the weekend, that a bunch of the guards had helped her move her things in. He said it was a nice place. Small but nice. He didn't know what she was doing for a job, though. He said that he guessed she was going to go to work for some company downtown."

Royce was going to find out. Just as soon as he hung up from this call, he was going to be making a few of his own. The woman had made him suffer long enough. He was finished waiting on her.

After telling his mom he'd let her know what he found out he called Daniel. Daniel said he'd need until tomorrow, but he'd get back to him. He wondered why he didn't ask why, but his phone was beeping again and he hung up.

"Mr. Hunter, it's Herman Gordon with the fire department. There's a fire at the old Benton warehouse. We were wondering if you could come down and help us out?"

CHAPTER 8

Leah was exhausted. Her head was pounding too. She put her untouched dinner in the sink and went into the living room to watch a little television and to relax. Maybe if she was lucky, her headache would stop hurting so bad and she could go to bed. She'd been tired all day.

She hadn't worked for several days. Her body was just too tired to make it out of bed and she hurt more and more when she simply moved from the bed to the couch. Tonight was the first time in a few days that she had been in the kitchen and she had made a mess of it. She'd get to it tomorrow, she decided, after she had a good nap.

There was nothing on the television so she turned it to one of those music stations and tried to mellow out. Chilled, she reached for the throw on the back of the couch and nearly had it over her when her hand went numb. Lifting her arm up, she looked at it and was frightened. Her vision was becoming blurred.

Terrified, she reached for the phone just as blood began to trickle out of her nose. She knocked the phone to the floor and only just managed to grab the handset before it too fell. She knew this was the end, knew she was dying. She needed to make just one more call.

Calling an ambulance seemed futile. She would be gone long before they got there and she'd not get to do one more thing before it was too late. Dialing blindly now, she hoped she pressed the correct buttons and didn't waste her last breaths on a stranger. When Kasey answered the phone, Leah wept a little.

"I love you." She felt the blood pour from her nose now and spill on her shirt. "I love you very much."

"Mom? Mom, what's happening? Where...oh God. Please, Mom, answer me. Tell me you're all right."

She hadn't meant to panic her, but Leah knew she would understand. "Be happy for me. You be happy. I love you."

"I love you too. Please don't die. Mom, I need you. Please, please tell me you're fine."

"I love you." The world seemed to still for a few seconds. Her body went numb all over and the phone slipped from her fingers. Nothing hurt, nothing hurt anymore, and she felt at peace. A bright light blinded her completely and then nothing.

Leah York died as peacefully as she could.

~~~

Royce got back to house at just after ten the next morning. His body ached and he smelled like smoke. The building had been completely engulfed by the time he'd gotten there and the fire department was trying to keep the fire from spreading when his family showed up. Arson, the chief said, gasoline had been poured over every floor and the place had gone up like dry tinder.

"You have any idea who would do something like this, Mr. Hunter?" the inspector had asked when it was clear it was intentional. "This kind of fire could have been a lot worse than it was."

"Yes, sir. Your men did a fine job keeping it contained. Who set it? I'm not positive. I have a few ideas, but nothing I can prove. And don't ask me. I won't tell you."

"Didn't think you would. You're brother, the lawyer, he said you and the previous owner had had words over what you had planned for the building. Thinking maybe it could have been him?"

Royce knew it was him, but didn't say anything. The inspector moved away after a few seconds. Royce had watched him stop and talk to his mom, but knew he'd get nothing from her either. Charles Benton had a lot to answer for and Royce was just in the mood to ask him.

When Royce stepped out of his bedroom after taking a long, hot shower, he tied off the trash bag he'd put his clothes in and took it to the trash can just outside the kitchen. The smell was as much a part of the material as anything and he knew he'd never get them clean. He was putting the lid back on the top when his mom pulled up.

"Hello, son." She sounded as tired as he did. "Got anything to eat in that monster kitchen of yours?"

He invited her inside and, while she started the pot of coffee, he gathered things to put together a nice lunch for them. He wasn't surprised when both his brothers showed up before the first pot was finished brewing.

"Do you think Charles was stupid enough to set the fire?" their mother asked as she bit into the large sub he'd made for them all.

"He probably didn't set it himself, but I'd bet any amount of money he was a part of it." Daniel got up and got them all a beer as he continued. "I have a few things to look into, one of which is the security cameras that I had installed. If they were up and operational before the fire we might have caught someone."

Royce nodded. "They're running. I got the okay to have them turned on the day before yesterday. I told them to run them now just in case."

Jesse looked up. "You thought he'd try something? Damn it, Royce, you should have said something. I would have had some of the security team out there."

"No, I didn't think he'd be that stupid. I was running it so we could see if we'd put the cameras in proper position. The company that installed them said they could come out and move the ones we wanted. I never thought of them until just now."

Royce hadn't thought of much anything the past few weeks and was beginning to think maybe he might have missed more than that. He looked up when Curtis' phone went off. He got up and left the room when he answered.

"I, for one, am exhausted, but I want to make sure that we are looking into this thing with Charles." His mom yawned for the second time in as many minutes. "Why don't we meet in the office—"

Curtis came back in and cleared his throat. "That was a guy I have looking into some things. Charles Benton was admitted to the hospital for smoke inhalation. He's on life support. It doesn't look that bad, but they don't want to take any chances."

Royce looked over at his mom when she started crying. "I never meant for him to go to such extremes. I…his daughter didn't deserve what he did to her, but I never meant for him to kill himself over some sort of revenge over this."

She finally lay down on the couch and covered up. Royce and his brothers cleaned up the kitchen without saying much more. They agreed to meet at the office tomorrow, go over the recordings from the fire, and turn them over to the inspector. After another hour they left and Royce went up to his own bed.

His plans to talk to Kasey were going to have to wait until tomorrow. He had to figure this out with Benton and see what they could do about the building. He was a little worried about this house and whether or not he'd set up someone to torch this one, but he'd also had a nice security system installed before he'd moved in. Royce was just drifting off to sleep when he remembered that he'd left his mom on the couch. She'd be fine, he knew, and fell into an exhausted sleep.

He'd slept around the clock he realized the next morning. When his alarm went off at six the next morning, he knew he'd never slept better. The quick shower and getting dressed for the office made him realize that he'd not felt this good about going to work in a long while. He was pulling up out front when he got his first of many calls for the day.

"The recordings are being delivered by courier this morning. There is some news on CNN about the fire that implicates Benton. And before you ask, no, I didn't let it leak." Royce laughed at Jesse. "Also there are four meetings today with some of the guys from the Maple Committee. They want some updates on whether or not you've decided to let investors come in or not."

"Why are you giving me updates and not Bobbie? I could have sworn that she did this every morning." He pulled into the parking place just as he asked. "Don't tell me you're my new secretary."

"Christ, no, but she called in. She said that there was a death and she needed to be there for them. She said something about it being a long time friend and if you wanted to dock her, she'd tell everyone where the bodies were." Jesse laughed. "I told her I might just do it to find out where you stuff them."

"I'm nearly in the building now. I'll see you when I get up there. I suppose you've got someone coming up to cover for her, right?"

"Yeah, two ladies are on their way up. I know you have just Bobbie, but this is going to be a hell of a day and I don't want anyone quitting on us right now. Oh and by the way, you have like forty messages on your machine."

Royce pulled out his badge and swiped it over the machine. The man at the desk didn't look familiar, but that wasn't anything new. The security team was expanding every day, it seemed, and they needed even more people. When the new buildings they had opening by the beginning of fall opened they'd be short staffed again. With a nod, he went to the private elevator and went to his office.

The messages were from the investors that Jesse had mentioned. Three of the men wanted in to "broaden their portfolio," another wanted to see about expanding his bottom line. They both meant the same thing, just one more honest than the other. He was fielding question about the Benton building when Curtis walked in with two other men. One he recognized from the fire, the other he didn't know.

"Let me get back with you on that. We're still checking the area out." He hung up on the man as he was sputtering about timelines. "What can I do for you gentlemen?"

"This is Inspector Gordon from last night and this is Fire Marshal Will Swanson. They have a few questions on the insurance we had in place. I tried to tell them it's a common practice for us, but Swanson here seems to think otherwise."

Royce simply got up and walked to the file cabinet against the wall. After a quick search, he came back with a handful of files. "There are the insurance policies that we have on each building we purchase. If you'll notice that on the day we sign the papers, we open a policy on the place. It's mostly for peace of mind, but also for the workers when they are on site. There are also attachments to each policy that we cancel. The reason, the date, and who did the closing. While I understand why you're asking, it doesn't mean I have to be happy about it."

They looked over the papers quickly. No one said a word and when they'd seemed to be satisfied, the two men left. Curtis hung around and said nothing for awhile. Royce knew his brother well enough to know that he'd say his piece eventually and when he did Royce knew it was going to be nothing he wanted to hear.

"Benton is going to make it. He confessed to the entire thing, including setting the fire on his own. He claimed it was because he was so grief-stricken, that the death of his daughter finally got through to him."

"Do you believe him?" Royce didn't. But he never had liked the guy in the first place.

"No. But it'll be a good defense. Temporary insanity over the death of his daughter is a good way to swing it. Finding out that we had plans to make the building as a tribute to her and he'd done nothing—less than nothing actually. He'll get off with some time, but not as much as he should."

Royce nodded. "And those idiots, what do you think they were doing if they knew he confessed? Looking for another angle for a friend?"

"No, CYA. It's always good, even when you have an ace in the hole to cover your ass. Like me covering yours for instance."

Royce didn't want to ask, but he did. "What have you done? And how much is it going to cost me?"

"The girl, in the off chance that she's pregnant, I've put together a contract that gives her a house and a car. Money to spend as she sees fit and a trust for the baby. All she needs to do is to leave you alone and never contact the family again. I also have one that says she'd entitled to nothing if she divorces you and that you keep the child. Either way, you're covered."

Royce shifted in his chair. He wasn't sure if he was supposed to be happy with what Curtis had done or pissed. He was feeling a little bit of both. Before he could answer, his brother stood.

"Or we can go with plan C. You tell me you love her beyond all your wildest dreams and I tear up both contracts and the two of you live happily ever after. It's up to you." Curtis walked to the door. "I'll see you tomorrow. If you need me or just want to talk, call. See you in the morning."

Royce was still sitting at his desk an hour later, no closer to figuring out what he wanted to do than he'd been before Curtis had come in. His personal line rang and he picked it up, smiling for the first time in days.

"I missed you today. The two girls we got from the pool to fill in for you didn't make my coffee right and they couldn't find anything I needed the way you did. Please tell me you're coming back tomorrow."

"I can come in tomorrow, but I'll need the next day off." Bobbie was quiet for a few more seconds than he liked. "I guess you didn't hear."

Royce sat up in his chair and closed his eyes. "I was told you had a death and that you needed to be off. Who was it? Not your sister-in-law, was it?"

"No. I thought...Leah York passed late yesterday afternoon. She'd been ill for some time and an aneurism took her life."

Royce felt the room tilt off its axis and then back again. He closed his eyes. Here he'd been plotting with Curtis the best case scenarios concerning her future and she was dealing with her mother's death.

"How's...Christ, I didn't know. How are they doing? Is...is Kasey all right? Jay, is he, is he handling this well?"

He heard her sob and his heart broke for his friend. "Jay is trying to keep them all together. Suzy of course doesn't understand, but she knows something is wrong. Kasey. Kasey is...I'm not sure. She won't...Leah called her when she was dying. She called Kasey and told her that she loved her and that she wanted her to be happy. When the ambulance got to her home, Leah had the phone on her lap and she was gone."

Royce stood up to leave. "Tell me where she is and I'm coming to her. I want to see her and..." And what? He sat back down hard in the chair.

"She was at her uncle's house when I left. I don't...I'm not sure if she was going to stay there or go home. She's taking it very badly. Then there was her father. He showed up right before I left. Kasey didn't move to speak to him, but I could tell she was upset."

"When is the funeral and where?" Royce didn't know if someone had sent flowers or not, but he would be there. "My family will be there for them."

"That's very nice of you, Royce. I'm sure they'll appreciate it. It's only a graveside. The poor dears haven't any money. It's at Cedar Cemetery on Wyatt Street. The paper said that the family would be there around one and that the service would begin at two or thereabouts."

Royce laid his head on his desk. He was an ass and he hated himself more in that moment than he had in his entire life. He sat up and spoke again to Bobbie.

"Let me know if I can do anything for them. Anything. I'm going to call my mom now, but you have my number if she…if they need anything."

"I will. You're such a dear boy. I know that they knew this was going to happen, but I don't think you're ever prepared. The poor girl and Jay…I don't think I've seen a man more devastated than he was today."

Royce called his mother when he got off the phone with Bobbie. "Mom, I have to tell you something. Can you meet me at my house? It's really important."

CHAPTER 9

Kasey sat in the chair near her mother's casket. Every time she looked at the daises decorating the top she felt tears slide down her face. She kept reaching out and running her hand over the top of the casket, wanting more than anything to have her mom back there beside her. She looked up when someone touched her arm.

"Hello, sweetheart. How you holding up?"

Kasey nodded and turned back to her mom. She didn't know who most of the people were who came to talk to her. Maybe she did, but she didn't care. She wanted them all to go away and leave her to her misery, but they just kept touching her and trying to have a conversation with her. She only knew one person she wanted to talk to and she wasn't speaking to her.

"Kasey, honey, can you please come back under the shelter? You'll get sick if you don't." Uncle Jay. She turned to look at him. "Come on, baby, you can't get sick. Let me help you pull the chair under the shelter."

She realized it was raining. Not a hard pour, but enough that she was getting soaked. Someone was standing next to him and she tried to stand, but she lost her footing in the wet grass and nearly tumbled.

"I've got you. Come on." She looked up into the face of Royce and tried to pull away. "Let me put you over here and then I'll let you go. Come on, Kasey, your uncle's right, you need to stay healthy."

"My mom is gone. She died and left me. She was doing so much better and now…what am I supposed to do now?"

He didn't answer her, not that she thought he would. He was there because her family…well, her uncle worked for him. It was nice of him to show up, but not necessary. She didn't want anyone there, as a matter of fact, and wished again that they'd go away.

She sat in the chair and looked at the casket again. The daisies where getting wet, she realized, and thought someone should cover them up. Then a small giggle escaped her mouth. They were flowers and needed to be wet. She looked up when someone stood in front of her.

Mrs. Hunter, Kasey remembered. She'd only seen the woman a couple of times. But she still remembered her. She stood up and took her hand. When she started to slip again, Mrs. Hunter steadied her.

"Why don't you have a seat, dear? You look all done in." She sat in the chair next to the one Royce had put her in. Kasey turned to look at the casket again. "I'm so sorry about your mother, Kasey. She was a nice woman."

Kasey turned to look at her. "You knew her? She never…at the Christmas thingy. She went with my uncle Jay last year. Yes, I remember now. She told me that you said she had on a pretty dress."

"She talked about you. She was so very proud of you. She told me that she couldn't ask for a better daughter."

Kasey started crying again. "I was a shitty daughter. She was alone when she died because I wanted my own place.

What kind of daughter turns down living with their mother when she knows she is going to die?"

"Stop that right now, young lady." Kasey turned to look at Mrs. Hunter. "You know better than that. She raised you to be independent and I doubt very much your mother was anything but happy for you."

Kasey felt herself being pulled into a warm hug and she lost the little control she had over her tears. She sobbed in earnest now, her heart broken, and feeling so lost she clung to the woman who held her until she had no more tears left. When she pulled away from her Kasey felt stupid and tried to move away as she apologized.

"I'm so sorry. I've had a bad few weeks. And my mother would be so...she'd be so unhappy with me if she could see what I've been doing." Kasey blew her nose on her damp tissue. "I thank you for just now. I didn't realize I needed that."

"Kasey," Mrs. Hunter said softly. "Royce told me what happened between the two of you. He said you and him have been fighting and that he wants to talk to you."

Kasey looked over her shoulder and saw him standing there with her uncle. He turned to look at her. Kasey turned back to the casket and felt her heart pound.

"Did he tell you what we've been fighting about, Mrs. Hunter? Did he tell you that...that there might be a child from our act of stupidity?" Mrs. Hunter said nothing and Kasey turned to her. "He...we won't marry if there is one. We both agree that...that it would be like pouring gas on an already out of control fire. I'm not sure if...I've been a little distracted about..."

"Kasey, I didn't...he said that you two had fought, but he never mentioned that he didn't...I'm sorry, dear. If there is a baby, I'll make sure he does the right thing by you and your child."

Kasey thought he was by not marrying her and turned to tell her so, but the reverend called the short service to order. Kasey barely heard what he said. Barely heard him telling the large gathering there that her mom was one of the sweetest people he'd ever known. That Leah York was proud of her family and that she'd be so embarrassed about the people gathered there to be with her. He went on to tell the congregation that there would be food and friends at Jay York's house and everyone was welcome. After a short prayer everyone but a few left for their cars while the family said their finally goodbyes. Kasey was still sitting in the chair when Royce came to sit beside her.

"Kasey? I told Jay I'd bring you to the house. Are you ready to go?" He took her cold hand into his warm one. "Baby, come on. You're frozen through."

"You told her. You told your mother that I might be pregnant. She pretended not to know, but she did, didn't she?"

"Yes. I told her last night. When I told her your mother had passed away, I said that I may have gotten you pregnant and that you and I had been fighting."

Kasey nodded. "But you didn't tell her you and I weren't getting married. She knows that now, but I don't think she believes me."

Royce didn't say anything for several minutes. And Kasey realized that the men were waiting for them to leave so they could finish up. She started to stand and he put his hand out to steady her.

"Don't touch me. Please, just…just don't touch me." She started to hobble away when she was suddenly lifted up in his arms. "Put me down right this minute."

"I'm going to carry you to the car and put you in it. Then we're going to stop at the closest drug store we can find and I'm going to buy a pregnancy test. We're getting this solved right now. It's been more than two weeks and we might know something. After that we'll have a calm and rational conversation and both of us will decide what we'll do if there is a baby."

She was suddenly in his warm car. When he reached across her and pulled the belt across her lap, she wanted to snarl at him to leave her alone, but she started to tremble and couldn't get the words out. By the time he came around to the driver's side, her teeth were chattering and she was shaking hard.

"Christ. You're in shock. Come on, Kasey." The blast from the heater hit her in the face and she felt something warm covering her. As she tried to get warmth into her body, she felt Royce begin to rub her leg.

"Cold. I'm so cold." She tried to stop her teeth from banging together, but all she managed to do was bite her lip.

"How long were you out in the rain? You're soaked through. I'm taking you home and putting you into a warm bath. Don't move."

Like she could. Her body's trembles made her dizzy and soon she was drifting in and out. She didn't think she should be doing that from just being wet, but was too cold to ask him.

She was lifted for a brief time then she heard someone swearing. When someone started tugging on her clothes, she tried to fight them back.

"Stop it. You have to get out of these wet clothes. I've called the doctor and he said to strip you down and put you in the tub. He said that once I get you warm to bring you in and he'll see about taking the bandages off permanently."

Kasey was too cold to care what he did, then suddenly she was burning up. When she tried to get away from the heat, he held her firmly while speaking to her. After what seemed like an eternity, she started to feel better. Soon, she drifted off into a deep sleep.

~~~

Royce held her until he was sure she was all right. Her body was lax against his, but still he held her in the tub for a little while longer. When he was sure she wasn't going to start shaking again, he stood up and took her into his bedroom.

He laid her on the floor, mindful about the soaking wraps on her arm and leg. His main concern was that she wasn't cold and that she seemed to be sleeping well. He wrapped two big towels around the wet elastic and then piled more towels on the mattress after he dried her off. He then put a large towel around her hair and picked her up. He put her into his bed and went to put on some clothes.

He'd worn his boxers in the tub with her and nothing else. His wet clothes were on the floor and he bent to pick them up as he dialed his mother. She answered on the first ring.

"Where the hell are you two? I've been worried sick that you'd had an accident on the way here. When are you coming?"

"She got a chill. Bad. I called Doctor Carmichael and told him what was happening and he told me to put her in a tub of water. My house was closer than hers so I brought her here. When she wakes up, I'm to take her into the emergency room and he'll make sure her injuries are all right."

"Is she all right now then?"

Royce looked down at Kasey's sleeping face. "I think so. She's sleeping. Mom, I'm sorry, but I'm not going to marry her. All we ever do is fight and I don't love her."

She didn't say anything for a few seconds. "All right. We should wait like you said to make any kind of arrangements for the child...if there is one."

He sat on the edge of the bed and watched her. He told his mom that he'd talk to her later and hung up. He brushed his fingers over Kasey's cheek and smiled at how soft it was. "Oh, Kasey," he said softly. "What am I going to do with you? You come into my life demanding that I badge in and set my entire world on its side. Now you could be carrying my child and all I can think of is whether it will have eyes the same as yours or your temper. And I don't even know if there is a kid yet."

Three hours later, he took her to the emergency room. The doctor decided that even though she was doing fine, he didn't like the sound of her lungs. He wanted to keep her for a bit longer. He also agreed to do a pregnancy test.

Royce was pacing the hall outside of the little room she was in when he saw the doctor. Doctor Carmichael had a straight face as he approached him so Royce wasn't sure if it was good news or...or something else. Royce started to follow him in the room when he stopped him.

"You can't hear the answer, Royce. The results are hers and hers alone. If she wants to tell you then that's fine, but you'll have to wait until then."

"But it's my kid. I have a right to know as much as she does." The doctor merely raised a brow. "Ask her. Ask her if I can hear."

"Okay, but wait out here until I ask her. I don't want it said that you forced her in any way."

Royce nodded.

It seemed so long from the time since the doctor left him in the hall until he came back out. But it was probably only a few seconds. Before he let him in, the doctor held him still.

"She said you can come in, but you're to keep your mouth shut—her words not mine. She said if you piss her off any more than you have, she'll hurt you. Do you understand?" Royce nodded, but the doctor wasn't finished. "This is from me. You make her cry and I'll castrate you. She's been through a lot in the past few days and I won't have you upsetting her. You understand that?"

"Yes, sir." Royce repeated that he understood and they went into the room.

She looked so pale lying there. He wanted to hold her hand, touch her in some way, but the way she was covered up, her arms under the blanket, screamed to leave her alone. He sat on the couch somehow knowing that either answer was going to be hard to take.

"You're pregnant, Kasey. If what you've told me is correct then you should be due right around the tenth of February. I can recommend a good doctor if you'd like or you can find one on your own."

Royce leaned back on the chair. Pregnant. Kasey was carrying his child. He stood up suddenly and then sat back down. He wasn't sure what to do.

"She's been...with all this going on, is the baby going to be all right?" He hadn't realized he's asked the question until they both turned to him. "I know it's early, but the stress, it won't hurt it, will it?"

Doctor Carmichael turned to Kasey before answering. "No, but I want you to try and rest a bit more. Get in to see a doctor as soon as you can. That'll start you off on the right foot. Do you have any questions, honey? This is a lot to take in."

"I'm fine. I'm…can I go home now? I want to go home now. Please." She sounded slightly panicky, but then took a deep breath. "I think I'll feel better about this after I let it sink in. I would like to go now, please."

"Of course. I would really like for you to stay, but I can understand that you need to be alone. You take a few days and get used to the idea. And let me be the first to congratulate you. You're going to be fine, Kasey, just fine."

The doctor walked out and left them, assuring them he'd have the nurse bring in her paperwork so she could get on her way. Royce stood up, walked over to her, and laid his hand on hers. She moved away.

"I want to go home. My home. If you're going to give me a hard time about it then I'll call a cab. I don't want to argue with you tonight." She turned her head away from him. "Tell me right now so I can call someone."

"I want you to come home with me, but I understand. But I'll come by tomorrow. We have things to discuss and how things are going to play from now on."

She nodded, but he wasn't sure she was listening. "Just take me home, please."

KATHI S. BARTON

CHAPTER 10

Kasey got up at just after eleven that night after tossing and turning for two hours. It wasn't like she wasn't exhausted because she was, but her mind simply wouldn't shut down. After fixing herself a glass of tea she pulled out her laptop and began looking things up and making herself lists. The first thing she searched for was a doctor.

There were over a dozen doctors in the immediate area, more if she wanted to travel a bit. While she was doing a rundown, she supposed it would be called, she started writing down questions she'd ask whomever she decided to go with.

She knew that Royce would help her if she asked—she was reasonably sure he'd insist, but this was her body and, for now, her baby. Giving the baby up for adoption was not completely out of the question, but it was low on the things to consider list. She wrote "adoption" on the top of another sheet with pros and cons after it.

The doctors she picked out from the list on the website she put on another sheet. There were three of them. She decided to call that doctor from the emergency room and ask his opinion. Also, she knew a couple of women from work who'd given birth recently and she was going to ask them as well.

By four in the morning, she had filled out three pages of questions and two more of things she needed more information on. Before she went back to bed she started another sheet with two more columns. The pros and cons of having the baby.

She wasn't going to abort, there wasn't even any question of her doing it, but there were other things to consider. Her living arrangements for one.

She knew she could live with her uncle and aunt. But did she want that? There was a lot to think about, like why she wouldn't, or what benefits she would gain, if any, if she did move in with them. Suzy would be the biggest issue.

She was used to being the center of attention. And the baby would be first and foremost in everyone's mind. Then there were the times that Suzy had temper tantrums, bordering on violent at times. Would she harm the baby, or even Kasey for that matter?

Kasey knew her current job would be okay with the baby hours. She could pretty much work whenever she needed to. But she was a realist enough to know she wasn't going to have enough money for the extras when the baby got older. Not that she knew what those would be, but she was sure they were expensive.

Kasey looked around her little one-bedroom home. Not enough room here either. Maybe at first, but later as the baby needed more equipment, she'd be hard pressed to put anything extra in the room, including a crib.

And what did she even know about babies? Nothing really. She had no brothers or sisters, not a single cousin, and had never even babysat for anyone's kids. She knew the basics, but nothing else.

Depressed, she went to her room. She'd decided that if she got a start on her work now, if she needed a nap later on today, she could be ahead of the game. After taking a good sponge bath, she got dressed in some comfy clothes and went back to the table correcting term papers and making corrections on quizzes she'd been asked to grade. It was almost seven when someone knocked on the door. She frowned when she saw Mrs. Hunter there.

"Hello, dear. I came to tell you how thrilled I am about the baby. I can't tell you how happy I was when Royce told me last night."

"I see. Well, thanks." Kasey didn't know what she should do now. Inviting her in seemed over the top to her, but apparently Mrs. Hunter thought differently.

"I was wondering if I could come in and speak to you about some things?" Kasey hesitated. "I won't be long, and I promise I'm not here to try and talk you into anything like marrying Royce. I want to, but I won't."

"All right," Kasey agreed, and opened the door wider and stepped back. She turned to gather her notes up, but a few of them dropped to the floor.

Bending was nearly impossible as sore as she was, so she was grateful when Mrs. Hunter helped her until she froze in place. She was staring at one of the lists she'd made. From her stricken expression, Kasey assumed it wasn't something she liked.

"I'm just making myself notes. I do better when I have things all lined up in neat little rows. I get more accomplished that way too."

Mrs. Hunter looked up from the paper into Kasey's eyes. "Are you giving the baby up for adoption? Or is this simply a threat you plan to use to get more money out of him?"

Kasey took a step back. Mrs. Hunter couldn't have hurt her more if she'd just slapped her. Putting all the notes, including the ones she jerked from the older woman's hand, on the counter Kasey went to the door. She was afraid to speak, so she simply held the door open. When Mrs. Hunter didn't move Kasey brushed at her tears and looked at her. "Get out."

"Kasey, I need to—" Mrs. Hunter started.

"I said to get the fuck out of my house."

When she finally moved toward the door Kasey braced herself for another blow—verbal or physical. She expected both if she was honest with herself, and actually looked forward to tangling with her.

"I didn't mean to say that. But you wrote it down. Women have done less to get money from a rich man and I made—"

"And you know me so well that you can believe something so vile, so horrible of me?" Kasey wiped again at the tears. "I'm very sorry that I'm not one of the elite women your sons are used to hanging around with. But I was born on the wrong side of the tracks, as well at the sheets, for that matter. I'm not Ivy League educated, but I worked hard for my education. I work hard, pay my taxes the same as the almighty Hunters. I'm even pretty sure I put my pants on the same as you too. If you want to treat me as less than you, fine. But know this right now, I will give this child up in a heartbeat if my choice is you people with your snotty airs rather than some guy who works forty hours a week and treats others with respect."

"Kasey, I—"

"I want you to get out of my house and never come here again. None of you. Just…I just want you to leave me the fuck alone."

Kasey closed the door gently after Mrs. Hunter walked out. After turning the lock Kasey went to her room and stretched out on the bed. Angry and hurt tears burned her eyes. Even as she rolled to her side she knew that she shouldn't have said those things. Royce would be pissed at her. Again. Kasey closed her eyes and tried to relax, but after laying there for two minutes she got up, hobbled to the bathroom, and threw up. After that she simply lay down and fell into an exhausted sleep.

~~~

Royce didn't know what to think. His mom had come into his office an hour ago sobbing. All he'd understood was Kasey, sheets, and something about blue collar workers raising and loving their families. It had taken him until a few minutes ago to understand what had happened.

"I hurt her so badly, Royce. The look...I shouldn't have said those things to her. I had no right to say anything to her. I should have just let you handle it as you said you would."

He didn't want to be pissed. He didn't want to be pissed at either of them, but as far as he was concerned both of them had handled this very badly.

"Mom, I'm sure that once Kasey thinks about it she'll realize that you meant her no harm." And if she didn't, he'd make sure she did understand. "By now she's probably thinking she overreacted and is sorry for the entire thing." Again, something he was going to make sure she saw.

But the adoption thing bothered him. Why would she immediately assume he wouldn't want to raise the child if she didn't want to? Of course he'd told her he didn't want to get married, but that didn't mean he couldn't hire someone to help him with his kid. It wasn't as though he couldn't afford it. Much better than she could, as a matter of fact. He'd been working on a budget for her when his mom had come in. Bobbie came in after a short knock.

"Oh, my, what's happened?" And that set his mom off again. Sometimes, Royce was glad he didn't live around a bunch of women. This was a prime example why he was going to remain single.

But Bobbie seemed to catch on a lot faster than he had. A woman thing, he figured. But Bobbie, for all her help in the office, was quick to point out what she thought about both him and his mother's faults. And there were plenty.

"Shame on you, Annamarie. That poor girl."

"Now see here—" Royce snapped at Bobbie.

"No, you see here. That girl just lost her mother, her best friend and the only person who's ever really loved her all in one shot. Then she finds out she's having a baby by a near stranger. You can't tell me that when you go to tear apart a business that you don't write down every single option, weigh all the options, and discard the ones you know won't work?"

"Yes. But this isn't a building, it a kid. And it's—"

"If you tell me that it's your kid, I will walk out that door and never return. It's not 'your' anything. It's the both of yours." Bobbie stiffened as anger seemed to pour from her. "No wonder the poor girl is thinking adoption is better. Just listen to the lot of you. You sitting there in that big chair of yours as if you haven't a care in the world telling everyone that you've no plans to marry the woman who is going to have your child. And you." She turned to his mom. "What did you expect her to do? Offer you tea and crumpets and be thrilled she's going to be a part of the exalted Hunter family? If she's smart she'll run as far and as fast as she can from all of you. She lost her mother, got pregnant, and you come and congratulate her." Bobbie slammed out of his office. Royce was speechless. But before he could regain his tongue and fire her, his mother spoke up.

"She's right. All of it. Even the tea and crumpets remark."

"Mom, I doubt you expected Kasey to make you a cup of hot tea and whip out some cookies for you. Or anything else."

"Yes, I did. Not literally, mind you. But I did expect her to be thrilled that she was having a Hunter. I also expected...well, to be honest, I expected her to be impressed. But she wasn't. She made no excuses. Hell, son, she wasn't even too happy about me being there at all much less in her house." She stood up. "But I'm going to do everything in my power to make it up to her. Starting with leaving her alone until she's ready to ask *me* for help."

"You'll see the baby, Mom. I won't let her keep it from you. And if she tries to put it up for adoption, I'll—"

"You'll what, Royce? Brow beat her? Steal the baby away from her as she's giving birth? Do you honestly think that's what you want? A child torn apart because you hate his mother so much?"

"I don't hate her. I just don't... You want me to marry her, don't you? Give the baby a father who doesn't want him?" Royce felt a sharp pain in his heart when he said that. He unconsciously rubbed the bruised area.

"No, I don't. You're so right in not marrying Kasey. It would be a major mistake even for you to make the offer to her." His mom opened the door to his office to leave.

"Mom, where are you going now?"

"To try and figure out how to repair the damage that I inflicted on an innocent woman and her child. Try to make at least some form of friendship between us so that neither she nor my grandchild will hate me."

CHAPTER 11

Daniel put down the phone and leaned back in his chair. Royce was going to be a father. Daniel had not seen that one coming. He still had a hard time believing it even after the second blood test confirmed it. Then the talk with Kasey— man, that was one pissed off chick.

He'd called her earlier to ask if she would mind going to see one of their doctors. He tried to explain that it was just to be positive, that doctors made mistakes all the time. But she wasn't buying it.

"And this doctor, because he's a Hunter-approved physician, he's above making mistakes, is that what you're saying? That only people handpicked by the rich are perfect?"

"No, I'm saying that I'd like for you to have it verified that you are indeed pregnant. So long as I get a report back from someone of authority saying yes, you had a test, and yes, you're pregnant, I don't care much who you see. I'm just trying to make it easy on you by making the appointment with a doctor I know. Plus, that way I can make sure the bill is paid." He knew the moment he'd said it, he'd screwed up again.

"Because as a regular person, a poor person, I don't pay my bills is what you're implying. I'll have you know that I pay all my bills, Mr. Hunter. I may not pay them all up front like you people do, but they do get paid," she practically snarled at him.

If his mother hadn't came in before he'd called Kasey and told him what had happened between the two of them, he might have snarled back. But he knew mostly why she was mad and didn't really blame her.

"Feel better?" he asked her. She didn't answer. "I find it's better to snap at the one who pissed you off, but I know that at times, like I'm sure it is for you now, it's not really feasible. Also, I use a punching bag, also probably not an option for you at the moment. I could bring you Royce and hold him down for you. Then you could wail on him all you want...just so long as I get a hit or two in on my own, you understand."

"And what about your mom? You going to hold her down for me as well? It could be a big day for the Hunters."

"Nah. With her, you're on your own. Don't tell her I told you this, but she scares the shit out of me."

Her laughter made him smile. "Thank you, Mr. Hunter, and if you'd like to start over, I think I can be nicer to you."

"You're very welcome, Kasey. And please call me Daniel." He picked up the list again. "I have a list of obstetrician-gynecologists for you. None of them have my approval because I don't usually deal with that sort of thing. But none of these have been under any investigation, nor have they been sued that I can find. Do you have a pen and paper?"

"Wait, I have a list of possibilities here. Read me your list and I'll go from there." He waited until she had her list. He knew she had one; his mother had told him she'd seen it too. He read off the names and she had all he had but one on her list as well. He had been impressed.

After she told him which two she was going to check into and gave him the one she'd see today, he told her he'd make the appointment but not pay the bill. She agreed to go in and have the test done as soon as she heard back from him.

"I'll have to wait on my uncle to come and get me. I still can't drive yet and he isn't home until after one today. I suppose I could call a taxi, but they're so expensive and I need to save my money."

Daniel thought about suggesting he'd send a car, but knew that she'd refuse. Besides, it wouldn't hurt to have Royce wait. Cooling his heels was just what Royce needed about now.

And now he had it confirmed. Kasey Marie York was going to have a baby. And next week, she'd have her due date and a full exam from a doctor of her choice.

Daniel realized that he couldn't wait to find out, couldn't wait to watch her grow large with his niece or nephew. And he couldn't wait for Royce to figure out what a fucking idiot he was.

He buzzed the idiot's office and smiled when he answered. "She's pregnant. The doctor said she's slightly underweight, but that was probably due to the extra stress. He said everything in her blood work came back just fine."

"Who is her doctor and how can I reach him? When is she going to see him again? I will want to be there so I can make sure she follows his instructions to the letter."

Daniel thought about taking a deep breath before he answered his brother. Or even stopping to count to ten. But he did neither. He just said what he wanted. "And you care why? I mean, you're a bottom line sort of guy, right? I understand that. But so long as the end product is how you think it should be, shouldn't that be enough for you?"

"What the hell is that suppose to mean?"

Daniel grinned again. Yeah, he needed a good fight and it looked like Royce was going to give him one. "The baby will be here and you, my dear, stupid brother, will be just as you are right now. Single, wealthy, and free to do whatever you want whenever you want. While Kasey can't."

"Why is everyone treating me like I've done something heinous to her? I made an error in judgment and now I'm going to be a father. It was just sex. I got caught up in the moment and forgot to use protection. How does that make me the bastard and her the injured party?"

Daniel burst out laughing without a bit of humor. "Wow, Royce, is that what you're going to tell your child? 'Sorry about your luck, kid, but I forgot to wrap my cock before I stuck it in your mother and you were the result of my lapse in judgment.' I'm sure you'll get father of the year." He slammed down the phone and left his office. If he stayed for one minute longer, he might decide to go and find Royce and beat the living shit out of him. Once for him and then again for Kasey.

~~~

Kasey told her uncle that she was pregnant. He'd been so angry at first. Not at her, but that the "boy" he'd called him, wouldn't marry her. She'd tried to explain that she wouldn't marry him for all the money in the world and that seemed to make him madder.

"What would your mom say? She'd be mad and you know it. She wanted the best for you and you being a single mom wasn't something she'd want for you."

"No, probably not. But she'd understand. And that's all I'm asking you to do. I don't know what I'm going to do yet. I know that whatever I do will be right for me and not for anyone else." She put her arms around him in a big hug. "I'm not asking you for help, Uncle Jay—"

"Well, you're going to get that anyway. Now, sit your bottom down and eat. I don't want to hear you aren't hungry either." He put enough food on her plate for ten people and told her to eat. They were just about halfway through dinner when he looked up at her. "You going to tell me who the father is or do I need to guess? I'm thinking it's that Hunter boy, but you tell me if I'm wrong."

"No, it's Royce Hunter. We had…it was right after I was hurt." She looked down at her plate, suddenly embarrassed. "He doesn't want me. He doesn't want anyone to be his wife. I'm not even sure he wants this baby."

Uncle Jay looked away. She could see that he was angry with her. Or so she thought. "Want me to talk to him? Actually, I'd really like to beat his ass. Will you let me do that for you? Please?"

She laughed at the pleading tone in his request. She'd almost feel sorry for Royce if her uncle wanted to go after him. But she shook her head. "No. You'd lose your job and then where will I be? If things get bad, I might have to come and live with you."

He brightened at that. "Why don't you? You can have your old room and I could redo that room next to yours. It's too small for anything but the storage room we've been using it for. I could knock out the wall and make it into a nice nursery for you and the little one." He looked shocked for a second. "Holy hell, I'm going to be a great uncle."

Kasey starting laughing and crying at the same time. "Yes, you are. And Suzy will be a great aunt. But I can't move in just yet. I need to…we need to get Suzy ready for this and me moving in might mess up her routine. You know how she is."

Uncle Jay nodded. "And she might hurt the baby. I never…you did, though, didn't you? She might not mean it, but she could. You're right. We'll have to work our way up with that."

Suzy spent most of her day in school. Even at her age, she needed the structure of doing the same thing every day and that included going to school. It also gave Uncle Jay a break and she was with someone who watched her very closely. He could work and not worry about her and she had her friends to play with.

Suzy was older than Kasey's mom had been and even Uncle Jay. She'd never been in a home and as far as Kasey knew, it had never been discussed. When her grandparents had died before Kasey was born, first her mom then Uncle Jay had cared for her. When Leah had been diagnosed with her brain tumor years ago Suzy had moved in with Uncle Jay and Leah had stayed in the house she'd rented Kasey's whole life.

At five-thirty when Suzy was dropped off from school they took Kasey home. And Kasey went to lie down and take a nap. She hadn't slept well the night before, not at all if she was honest, and she was tired. She needed to be up early the next morning because her phone was being installed and she had over two hundred pages to correct before Friday, which gave her three days.

Her nap ended up being fourteen hours long. She woke refreshed and rested. At just after eight-thirty the phone serviceman knocked on her door and she told him where she wanted the jacks. When he left at just a little over an hour later she pulled out the phones she'd picked up cheap.

Her cell phone was too expensive to use for everyday since she paid by the minute, so having a house phone was going to save her money. She called and gave the number to her uncle and then the school where Suzy went. She didn't know anyone else that would want it or that she talked to all that much so she went back to work on the papers. She didn't even think of the time passing until someone knocked on her door and she saw that it was just after two in the afternoon. She nearly went back to her little table when she saw who it was.

Opening the door she blocked Royce from coming in. "I don't want to see you. I'm having a really good day and you'll just fuck it up."

"I want to see what you found out at the doctor's. My brother thinks it's funny to keep any information I may need about you from me."

Kasey decided that she really liked his brother. "I don't know what information you think you might *need* about me, but I don't have any to give you. I don't have a doctor's appointment until…until later, and it's really none of your business anyway."

She still had the door blocked and he looked around the hall at the lady who came out of her apartment. "Can I please come in? This is really stupid to have a conversation out where everyone can hear us."

"No."

He looked ready to explode and she wanted to smile. But she was afraid if she did, he really would have a fit. When he pulled out his wallet, she stiffened. If he pulled out even one dollar, she was going to shove it up his nose.

"I have some phone numbers for you. Just in case. I put all my brothers' there and my mom's too. You have the office number, I guess. Anyway, call me when you need something."

She took the card and put it in her pocket without looking at it. "And what is it you think I'll need from you, Royce? I think I've made it perfectly clear what I want, and in case I didn't, I'll tell you. Nothing. Not one thin red penny. I have a lot of decisions to make and—"

"I have a right to know what you're planning. It's my kid too, you know. I have the right—"

"You gave up those rights the moment you told me that you thought what we'd done was an act of stupidity. Oh, don't get me wrong, I was just as guilty of that act as you. The only difference is I'm willing to own up to what I did. You want to wallow in self pity."

He braced his arms over his chest. "So now you think we should get married, right? You've thought it over and now you want to have a ring on your finger and a daddy for your kid."

She threw back her head and laughed. "You arrogant asshole. I wouldn't marry you if you were the last man on earth. Don't come here again. Ever. Do you understand me? If you do then I'll get a restraining order against you so fast you won't even have time to call in a favor. Now get out." She slammed the door. She watched him jump back as the door shut, disappointed that it didn't pop him in the nose. She went to her desk, sat down, and looked at the numbers he gave her. She picked up the phone before she had time to think and dialed the fourth number.

"Daniel Hunter? This is Kasey York. Would you like to get some pizza with me?"

CHAPTER 12

Royce was standing outside Curtis' office the next morning when he got in. Royce had actually thought about going to see Daniel, but he was still slightly pissed off at him. And his mom was in a meeting.

"I need to speak to you," he said to his brother as soon as he stepped off the elevator. "Kasey isn't giving me any choice so I need to do something so I have information about the baby."

Curtis unlocked his door and went inside. He hung up his jacket and checked his messages, completely ignoring him. Finally, Royce snapped. "Damn it, I'm talking to you. Fucking quit screwing around and answer me."

"Okay," Curtis started. "You didn't ask me a single question but barked information to me. Second, that's a personal issue, not business. And while I did suggest you make a contract with Kasey to ensure your rights, I've since changed my mind. Third, I—"

"Did Daniel talk to you? Is that what this is about? I see he's gathering you all together to make some sort of Anti-Royce Club. Well, I'm not going to marry her. I—"

"Good. I hope to God you don't."

That shut him up. He knew he would regret asking, but found he really wanted to know. Before he could ask, Curtis continued.

"We had dinner with Kasey last night. And before you ask, no, we didn't go behind your back. She asked us. Well, she asked Daniel. Jesse and I went along because we were in his office when she called him."

"Why? Why did she want to ask Daniel? To get you guys to be more pissed at me?" Royce felt stupid as soon as the words left his mouth.

"Will you just listen to yourself? Christ, Royce, you sound like you're ten years old and nobody will let you into their club. We had pizza with her. She wouldn't let us even mention your name or we had to leave."

That bothered Royce too, but not in the same way. It seemed Kasey was going out of her way to have nothing to do with him. Small wonder, he thought. He was being...well, he realized last night he was being just plain mean to her. "So what did you talk about? Is she...Curtis, do you think she needs... I was going to ask if she needed me, but I think she made it pretty clear she doesn't. At least not me, she doesn't."

Curtis laughed. "That's the first thing you've said in a month that's true. At least partly true anyway. I think she'll do well as a single mom. Her mom raised her pretty much on her own while helping care for Kasey's aunt. And I think Kasey will make a terrific mom."

Royce looked at his brother and said what he'd realized last night. "She'll do a better job without me. Don't say anything," Royce told him when Curtis started to speak. "I've been a complete and total ass with her. No, that's not true either. I've always been an ass."

"You're not going to hear me disagree with you," Curtis said, laughing. "I love you, but damn, man, you're not nice sometimes."

"Thanks," Royce said without heat. "The thing is, she makes me crazy, not because she's going to have my baby, but because she's not the least bit impressed by me."

Royce flushed when Curtis laughed again. "You mean she doesn't worship the ground you walk on? Well, no wonder she makes you cranky."

Royce started pacing. "Yesterday I went by to see her and she wouldn't even let me in her apartment. She made me stand in the hall like...like an unwelcome guest. I suppose I was. And she told me if I came around again, she was going to get a restraining order against me. Nor does she want my money."

"She probably doesn't need it. Not now in any case. I gave her the money she had coming to her from her paychecks last night."

Royce turned to look at him. "What money? I thought I'd already given her that money." And he'd found out she'd used it to pay off her mother's hospital bills and her funeral services. Bobbie had told him that yesterday. Apparently Leah had had no insurance before she'd been diagnosed and no one would insure her afterwards.

"She's on medical leave, injured on the job. I figured you wouldn't mind if she got her full checks at an average of the hours she'd been working for the past year. Minus the insurance policy, of course." Curtis handed him a sheet of paper. "I don't know much about babies, but that should cover most of the costs."

Royce looked at her weekly hours. She'd averaged seventy-nine hours per week. "She must have been happy about this." Then he frowned. "No, she was probably pissed off and gave you a hard time for even suggesting that she take it."

"Pretty much. She said she couldn't say no about all the overtime, not with White holding the full-time position in front of her like a carrot. She said that every time someone would get hired in, he'd tell her they had more experience or some such bullshit."

Royce nodded. "I suppose you've looked into any others he might have done this to. Was he abusing anyone else?"

"Yes," he answered softly. "Four others. All women. I've contacted two of them, the other two I'm still trying to find. I was going to talk to you today about it. How do you want it handled?"

"The same as with Kasey. Also...give them some sort of bonus. You decide on the amount." Royce sat back down. "Is she all right?"

Curtis smiled. "She's wonderful, funny, brilliant. I don't know when I've had so much fun. But she's also very...no, she's brutally honest, headstrong, and mouthy. Much like you, in fact. We were talking about it on the way home, how the two of you are the perfect match for each other and think it would be a mistake if you two were to marry. You'd kill each other within a month."

Royce went to his office a little while later. He had plenty of work to do and several projects he needed to get started. Curtis got him updated on the Benton fire and what was happening there.

The Benton estate, seized because the fire was arson, was going to pay for the building to be replaced once the funds were able to be used by the shareholders. Plus, they were going to add an additional one million dollars in contributions. Neither knew where the funds were coming from, but were pleased with the outcome.

The case against White wasn't finished because of the additional information from Kasey and the other women. Curtis said they were opening themselves up for a little backlash, but he thought it would be all right. The firm contacting the women instead of the other way around would make them look better. Royce said he was worried less about image at this point and more about making things right. Curtis agreed.

Curtis also gave him some advice. "If you want to be a part of your child's life, then I suggest you man up and shut up. She doesn't need you, or any of us for that matter. But she does need a friend. When we had dinner last night, she let it slip that she's lonely, that she doesn't have anyone she can just call. The three of us, Daniel, Jesse, and I, all volunteered. You could be on that list too."

Royce wanted that, he thought, but before he could say so Curtis continued. "But if you hurt her, drive her away, or even make her shed one more tear, we've decided we will hunt you down and hurt you in ways you can't even imagine."

Now Royce sat at his desk over an hour later. His screen had gone black and the pen he'd been holding had stained the blotter beneath it. He had to toss away four sheets of otherwise blank paper to hide what he'd done while he'd been deep in thought. Taking a deep breath, he picked up the phone before he changed his mind and dialed her cell phone.

"Kasey, it's Royce Hunter. Please don't hang up. I'd like to talk to you please."

~~~

She closed her eyes. She didn't think he knew how to simply talk. Bark, give commands, but not talk.

"All right," she answered him finally. "But you piss me off again and I'm hanging up."

"Okay, I understand. I wanted...I want...shit, Kasey, I'm an ass and I'm sorry. For everything."

Kasey looked at the phone then put it back to her ear. "Okay, who is this and what have you done with Royce, the real Royce Hunter? You know, the one who snaps orders and demands results." She was only half kidding, but he apparently took her seriously. She could hear the shame in his voice.

"I deserved that. And more. I've been a royal pain in the ass since I met you. My secretary is barely civil to me, my brothers have threatened to have me murdered, and my own mother is ready to have me kidnapped and taken to another country never to be heard from again."

That pissed her off. "And I suppose that's my fault too. Look, if you called me up so you could make nice with your friends and family, that is so not my problem. I have—"

"Christ, will you take it down a notch? I didn't say it was your fault, damn it. I was just telling you that... Hell, I don't know. I just wanted you to know you're not the only one I've made mad lately."

She nearly laughed at his beaten tone. But she wasn't ready to forgive and forget just yet. If she ever would be ready. "Why did you have sex with me that night?" The question was out before she could sensor it. He was quiet for so long she didn't think he'd answer. But when he did, she wasn't sure how to deal with it.

"Honestly? I'm not sure. I wanted you. When you stopped me in the lobby that morning I thought you'd be fun—someone to have some dinner with and maybe, if I was lucky, a good lay."

"Gee thanks. I'm trying to do my job and you're only impressed with my bust size and a piece of my ass."

"You know, I just realized I've never even seen your breasts. Never touched my mouth to your lovely flesh. I want to do that right now, Kasey, very much so."

The silence was profound. Kasey wasn't sure if she wanted to laugh or brain him. "Perhaps we should move on to something else," she said to him. "I don't even know why you called."

He didn't say anything for several seconds and she was sure he was going to go back to the subject of her breasts, but he didn't. She listened to him as he told her the rules she was going to have to follow and she had no idea why she thought he'd written them down. She decided to test her theory.

"What was number four again?" Like she cared, but it was the last one she'd written down when he started reciting them.

"Number four? Oh, let's see…oh, you're going to have a checking account that I will provide—"

"You did write them out. What did you do, sit at your desk all morning and make up this list of things you wanted to dictate to me and thought that I'd just simply do them?"

"Yes. And why wouldn't I? It's just as much my responsibility as it is yours. And that being said—"

"Yes," she snapped at him. "That being said, I'm *not* your responsibility. You'll either back off or I swear I'll bean you the next time I—don't you have anything else to do other than drive me crazy? Some old peoples' home to foreclose on or something?"

"I do not foreclose on things, especially not retirement homes. Why won't you ever let me finish a sentence? You are forever cutting me off when I'm trying to—"

"You never try to do anything. You simply put out your demands then sit back while other people hop to it. And if you said anything that I wanted to hear, then maybe I'd listen to you." She sat up straighter in her chair before continuing. "If and when hell were to freeze over then maybe, just maybe, I'd come to you for help. But until then...fuck the hell off." She closed her phone up and laid it on the table. She was so tempted to throw it at the wall and watch with great satisfaction when it shattered, but knew that she'd be the one to clean it up and then she'd have to replace it. She picked up her mug. The temptation to destroy it was nearly overwhelming. Instead, she put it down and burst into tears. She was contemplating screaming when her house phone rang.

"Miss York, it's Doctor Miles' office. We wanted to confirm your appointment for tomorrow."

Kasey laid her head on the table and listened to the woman tell her what she'd need to bring, all the while wondering if she was going to be delivering in prison or not. Murdering Royce Hunter was becoming more and more tempting every day.

CHAPTER 13

"Are you even listening to anything I'm saying to you?" Royce looked over at his brother. "You're not, are you? Damn it, I've been talking to you for seven minutes and you've been—"

"You timed me? You actually know it was seven minutes. Who does that?" Royce watched Curtis flush. "You didn't. Then how did you even come up with seven minutes?"

"I was guessing. And like you care. Where were you just now or do I even want to know?"

Now it was Royce's turn to flush. "I wasn't anywhere. Now, what was this you were saying about the last quarter? I'm listening now, so let's get this meeting finished."

Royce felt himself drifting off again ten minutes later. His brother apparently noticed it too. "Okay, tell me what the hell is going on with you. I'm not going to waste any more of my time if you're going to be in la-la land the entire time."

"Kasey won't tell me anything." Christ, he sounded ten. "I tried calling her about when the appointment is and she won't answer her phone."

"I hate to sound like a broken record here, but again, why do you care? She's a grown woman who knows how to take care of herself. I'm sure she'll do fine by the kid too. You've made it perfectly clear to her and everyone else who'll listen to you that you aren't interested in her or the baby. So either move on or change the way you act."

But he did care. Not that she hadn't made it easy for him not to; he was beginning to care very much. He looked over at his brother. Did he want to open that can of worms with him? Yes, he decided that he did.

"I want to start over with her. I know that it sounds lame, but I want to take her out, maybe go to a movie or something. I don't...I haven't a clue how to do that. I'm afraid that I've pretty much made it so she won't ever speak to me again." He looked over at Curtis, wondering if he thought this was funny. "I don't even know when her birthday is."

"January tenth, I saw it on her application. Why? I mean, if it's the baby, I can probably persuade her to let you have visitation rights. If she keeps it. And before you blow up about that, she's only looking at all her options, not making any decision just yet."

Royce got up and started pacing the room. "I don't have any real concrete reasons. She has a smart mouth that both irritates and intrigues me. She's very beautiful, though that isn't all of it. She's headstrong and smart, she is passionate and funny. I actually find myself wondering if the kid will have her temperament and hope that it does."

Curtis cleared his throat before he spoke. "Are you in love with her, Royce? Or is this just a case of having something that's been denied you?"

Royce nodded. He understood what his brother was asking. "I'm not in love with her. I like her, I understand her...well, most of the time. She makes me think of things I'd never... Are you aware that her mother raised her without any support from Kasey's dad?"

Royce had called a private investigator and had a thorough search made on the entire family. Jason York and Susan York included. He'd found out a great deal, more than he'd ever thought about the little family.

"Yes. Her father is making demands on her. He wants whatever insurance policy money that Kasey had from her mom's death. He seems to think his daughter is holding out on him."

Royce hadn't known that. "Is he threatening her?" Curtis nodded. "Will he hurt her, you think? I'm sure you've done something about it, right?"

"No. She won't let me. And believe me, I tired. I had someone watching her place up until she had the guy arrested for a peeping tom. Then the next night she pulled a gun on the next guy. Scared the shit out of him too. I had an ex-Navy Seal in my office telling me how scary it was to have this little bit of a thing holding a gun to his head and his nuts. He said she even fired the gun at his groin and told him that next time the gun would be loaded."

Royce laughed. It wasn't really funny, but he could see her doing that. Curtis reached into his briefcase, pulled out a file, and threw it on the desk.

"That's her medical record from the doctor she's seeing. If you tell her I gave them to you she'll stop the information. If you even hint that I'm helping you, I'll make your life not worth living."

Royce opened the file and looked up at his brother. "You'll help me? You'll help me try and make it up to her?"

Curtis stood and took his case with him. "For now anyway. I like this girl. I didn't want to, but I do. She's agreed to let me go to her next doctor's appointment. They were going to do an ultrasound, but she can't afford it. And before you claim that you'll pay for it for her, I think you really should rethink that. She's very…proud, and anyway, I don't think she'd take the money from you. I'm guessing you have about two weeks to try and see if you can convince her you want to be there too."

After Curtis left Royce started reading the file. He was on the second page when he started making notes. Not notes like he normally did when he decided he found something he wanted, but notes on things he wanted to remember. Things like her birthday and her age. He made notes about the schools she'd gone to and the awards she'd won. The colleges she'd attended and what her grades were like. He'd even made notes on the type of places she'd visited and a mental note to ask Curtis how he'd found out. By the time he was finished, he had a better understanding of her. Not a lot, but enough to maybe get him on her better side. He picked up the phone and started on "Plan Kasey."

"Hello, I'd like to order some daisies to be delivered." And the first thing he had to do was grovel.

~~~

The knock at the door startled her from a nap. She'd been working on a term paper for someone and it had been so boring that she'd fallen asleep correcting it. She had no idea what the paper was supposed to be about. Something about hamburger, of all things, and what medicinal properties it had. She hoped this person failed.

She opened her door to a bunch of daisies. Not just the run of the mill white ones, but brilliantly-colored ones too. Also baby's breath and greenery wrapped up in a large ribbon and a big vase.

"Miss York?" the man holding the flowers asked her. Her squeal of delight made him laugh. She'd never received flowers before and was so excited she grabbed them out of his hands before she even acknowledged him.

"Yes, that's me," she finally told him. "Oh aren't they lovely, all happy and colorful? Who are they from?"

She was searching for a card when he told her he didn't know but could she please sign? Taking the little clipboard and the flower-looking pen, she scribbled her name. She put the flowers down without finding a card when she went to find her purse.

"The tip has been taken care of," he told her when she tried to hand him five dollars. "You have a good day."

After closing the door and locking it, she pulled the little envelope out that was buried deep within the over three dozen blooms and read it. She was still sitting there holding the card when her phone rang.

"You like them?" Royce asked her. She looked at the card again. "Kasey? Are you there?"

"You sent me flowers. Why?" She flushed when he laughed. "I mean, they're lovely, my favorite actually, but I don't understand the message."

"I wanted you to know that I was thinking of you, that's all. You like them then? I'm glad. The lady at the flower shop was sort of cranky about getting them to you today."

"Were you demanding? That always puts my back up. Maybe you should try asking instead of demanding. It might get you more help than hindrance." He laughed again and she found herself smiling. He had a great laugh and she wondered why he was— "What's happened? You're not usually in this good a mood when you talk to me. You're up to something. Spill it."

"I'm not up... I guess I deserved that. I just wanted to send you some pretty flowers. And the first thing I thought of was daisies. And the reason I called is I have a favor to ask you."

"See, I knew it. I haven't made up my mind on the baby yet. So if that's all you called about then—"

"That's not it either." He sighed heavily. "I need a date tomorrow night and I was hoping you'd agree to go with me. It's a charity function...some sort of art show that the committee I'm on is throwing to kick off the new art gallery."

She still didn't believe that there wasn't something else so she didn't agree just yet. "Who's the artist and what's the media? And what's the dress code?"

"Media? You mean the type of art? Let me see...I just had the invitation... It says here 'come and help us celebrate the grand opening of the Hunter Art Group. Buy and appreciate the work of renowned artisan Paul Gleason. Mr. Gleason and his collection of raku fired stoneware and his fine work in porcelain will kick off...' Christ, this sounds like something my mother would set up."

She laughed at his tone and wondered if he had any idea about this before today. "I'm sure it sounds like fun. Isn't there anyone else you'd rather take and bore to tears?"

"No. It's black tie. I'm sure they don't expect you to wear a tie...though that might be kind of fun, but I'll pay for your dress. And before you get yourself in a twist about it, I can take it off my taxes. I'll call is a business expense."

She wanted to go. She'd actually heard of Paul Gleason and his work. In college he'd been a visiting artist and she'd had to work that night and missed his lecture. She was nearly ready to say yes when he spoke again.

"Daniel and Curtis will be there. I think my other brother Jesse will as well. I don't know if they'll have dates, but they have to come too." She heard someone speaking. "Okay, Daniel and Curtis have no date, Jesse has two, and my mom will be there."

His mom. She was probably still pissed at her. Well, if she did keep the baby, she would probably have to play nice with his family so she thought she should start now. She didn't particularly want to go with Royce, but with the others there she thought she might have a fairly good time. "All right, I'll go with you, but I'm not your date. I'm just your...escort. And not the hourly type either. I want to see Mr. Gleason's work and that's all."

She heard him take a deep breath. "Great. I'll...how will you get a dress and me pay for it? If you want me to go with you to help pick it out then—"

"I'm quite capable of purchasing a dress, Mr. Hunter. But I will let you send a car to pick me up. I have a car, but I'm sure it isn't what the hoity-toity people you hang around with are used to."

"All right then. I'll have a car at your house at four-thirty. My brothers and I are meeting for dinner at Muddy Misers. That way if this thing runs late, we won't be starving to death afterwards. The dress. I can leave my credit card with Bobbie Noel. She said you know her."

She wasn't sure what else to say to him so she simply hung up. Now what? She really didn't have a clue how to buy a dress. She pulled up images of exhibits on her computer and realized she was in over her head. After waiting one hour, she called Bobbie.

"I was wondering if I could ask you a favor. I need some help buying a dress for that art thingy with Mr. Hunter and I didn't want him to know I don't have a clue what to do."

"If you'll hold for one moment I'll get that information for you. It has been a hectic afternoon and I'm straightening out some last minute things with my boss before I leave for the day. Could I meet with you at say...six-thirty?"

"He's there, isn't he? Okay, you'll meet me at my house then? Or my uncle's? Either is fine by me."

"Hummm, how about yours? I can see to that and anything else you may need while I'm there."

"All right. I'll see you then." Kasey hung up smiling. She really liked Bobbie and was happy for her friendship. She also thought that she was sweet on her uncle and neither of them seemed inclined to do anything about it. She thought maybe she'd do a little matchmaking while she was at it.

At seven o'clock that night Kasey was looking at dresses. She decided that this was perhaps the stupidest thing she'd ever done. She hated that this thing was going to cost a fortune and they hadn't even found a dress yet. She was just going through yet another line of dresses when she saw it.

The dress was beautiful. Not just beautiful, but sinfully so. It was a black silk sleeveless gown that she knew would fit her. She glanced at the size as she pulled it from the line of dresses and realized that it was going to be too large, but nothing that couldn't be fixed. She hung it on the hook to see the whole effect when Bobbie came up behind her.

"Oh, my dear, that's it. Please tell me that you plan to try that one on. It'll make Royce drool all night."

She didn't comment on Royce drooling. "It's very…sexy, isn't it? I mean, it's not too much? Or I guess too little, is it?" Kasey turned to look at Bobbie when she laughed.

"That's the point, sweetheart. Try it on. If it doesn't look good on you then we'll keep looking. But I don't think we'll need to. I'm going to go over here to find some shoes to go with it."

CHAPTER 14

Royce knocked on her door. He was a little early, but not too much. He glanced at the woman who stepped out when he walked up the hall. He nodded to her and started to knock again when the door was opened. Bobbie was standing there with the strangest look on her face.

"She's not coming, is she?" Bobby nodded her head. "Then what are... She called you to help her?"

"Yes. She didn't want you to know, but I helped her pick out her dress yesterday too. You are a little early so have a seat. She'll be out in a couple of minutes. Your brothers are not with you?"

"In the limo. She didn't have any trouble, did she, with the card, I mean? I called the bank and told them she was going to use it. They told me that they'd make sure that she didn't—" He turned around when Bobbie nodded to his left. "Holy fuck."

The woman standing just behind him was a vision. He couldn't believe how different she looked. And how beautiful. The dress, what there was of it, was...stunning.

It was black silk and hugged her body like it had been painted on her. Her left shoulder was bare all the way to her wrist while her right had a bejeweled strap just over her shoulder that held the form-fitting bodice up. The entire left side from just below her breast to her hip was open with small scalloped edging that was held together with three more straps that wrapped around her like the one over her shoulder. The dress hugged her hips and fell to the floor in a waterfall of clinging silk. When she turned around he could see that her back was bare as well with only the straps as coverings. He whimpered. He was in so much trouble here.

He suddenly found himself standing before her. "You're beautiful. Stunning. Words fail me."

She grinned up at him. "You seemed to do all right there. Bobbie said it would make you drool. I've never owned anything so decadent before. Do you think I'll look all right?"

For an answer, he gently pulled her to him and kissed her. He didn't want to muss her, but the moment her mouth opened under his he knew that he had to have more. He pulled her to his body and deepened the kiss.

Her mouth was warm, soft, and wet. He touched his tongue to hers and he felt her moan. Royce wanted to devour her. He wanted to run his hands up her waist and feel her breasts fill his hands. He wanted to see what she had on beneath the gown and taste her. He wasn't sure how much longer they would have gone on if someone hadn't poked him—none too gently—in his back. He turned to look at Bobbie.

"You're going to be late if you keep that up. And I'm sure your mother will be very upset with you if you are." Bobbie handed him a swath of material then took it from him. He was glad because he was drawing a complete blank on everything but Kasey.

They were suddenly walking to the door. He was happy to see that Kasey looked as dazed as he did. When they were ready to open the door he looked down at her again. He realized then that the material had been a cape of sorts. He was both glad and disappointed that she was covered up. He wanted to hide her away from what he was sure was going to be every male in the gallery and he wanted to admire what was all his.

The trip to the gallery was noisy. His brothers kept a steady stream of conversation with Kasey and him, mostly Kasey. She laughed and joked with them as if she'd known them forever. Royce tried his best not to appear jealous, but he was. He found himself wanting to pound his brothers and then do it again. When the limo slid to a stop they got out ahead of them. When Jesse started to reach in for Kasey, Royce knocked his hand out of the way.

"Hey, I was just trying to help a pretty lady." Royce glared at him as Jesse winked at him.

"Take care of your own dates, thanks. This one is mine." Royce flushed when he turned to see Kasey out of the limo and staring at him. "Are you ready?"

His tone was sharp and he knew that she'd heard it. He wanted to tell her he was sorry, but they were being ushered inside by the doorman. When he reached to take her wrap, she stepped away from him. He wanted to roar with frustration, but knew that would only make him look stupider. He needed to make this right, but wasn't sure how.

"Oh my God," he heard Curtis whisper just behind him. "Christ, she's going to cause a riot. It's hard to believe she's pregnant."

Royce nodded and reached for her. When she started to step away again he pulled her to him. "I know you're mad at me, but I need to touch you," he said close to her ear. "Please, I'm so sorry for what I said, but...well, I was jealous. I didn't mean to embarrass you."

Before she could answer him his mother came up beside them. She took one look at Kasey and nodded. Royce wasn't sure what it meant, or for that matter why she approved, but he didn't ask. He was in enough trouble tonight and he didn't want to end up on the wrong end of a gun. He wasn't sure where Kasey might have hidden one, but he wasn't willing to find out.

They wandered around together for about twenty minutes when someone needed to speak to him. As much as he hated to leave her, he had to. She still hadn't said anything about his comment about being jealous. He left her in one of the front rooms with a promise he would return as soon as he could. He brushed his mouth over hers before he left.

~~~

Kasey looked at the work in front of her without really seeing it. She was still trying to wrap her head around Royce being jealous. Of her? She couldn't figure out why he'd say something like that unless it was to warn his brothers off. Off what she couldn't figure out, but that was the best she could come up with.

"I don't think I've ever seen anyone look at art quite like that before. Do you like it or are you trying to figure it out?"

Kasey turned to smile at the man beside her. "It's very lovely. I love Mr. Gleason's work. I think his work with porcelain is my favorite, but this is amazing. I love the cobalt blue glaze." And it was pretty, she realized as she turned back to look at it. "I don't know a lot about raku firing, but this is an amazing piece."

"Raku firing? Isn't that a different process of kiln firing pots? I remember now, the pieces are removed from the kiln at a high temperature and then something happens and the body starts to craze, I think it's called. It immediately starts fracturing when the pot is removed from the heat." She nodded. "I don't know a whole lot about this stuff. I just know that my late wife enjoyed the arts and I come because she liked them so."

Kasey thought there was more, but didn't comment. When she moved to the next piece, he walked with her. Kasey didn't mind. There were enough people around if she got into trouble, but she really didn't think she would. He seemed like a very lonely nice man.

"I'm actually here to see your boyfriend." She must have looked confused. "Royce Hunter. He wants to buy my building and I...I have to sell, but I just don't want to. It was my first business that my wife and I put together."

"Mr. Hunter isn't my boyfriend. We can barely tolerate each other under the best of circumstances. I'm just his date because I love this man's work." She wasn't going to think about Royce being jealous, nor was she going to think about the kiss he'd given her before they'd left her apartment. "If you don't want to sell then why are you?"

"Because he's not giving me a choice. He's forcing me out and all my employees are going to not have a job as soon as I sign the papers." His voice was bitter. She turned to look at him when he apologized.

"Forcing you out? I don't know...is that a normal way to do business? I've worked with Mr. Hunter for years and I've never known him to force anyone out before." Which was true. She'd only been on his security team, but she was reasonably sure that didn't sound like him.

The man seemed to take several deep breaths before he looked at her. "I didn't...he's not. I'm a bitter man. I'm sorry, miss. I shouldn't have..." He started to walk away.

"Wait. Don't leave. Tell me why you said that. It's a horrible thing to say about someone and you don't strike me as the type to say things like that normally. Please, come back and tell me." He stood staring at her and she thought she'd gone too far. "I'm Kasey York. You're…?"

"Fredrick Klingner." He smiled at her. "You're a very beautiful and smart woman. Does Royce appreciate you? If he doesn't, you come to me and I'll straighten him out."

They talked for another hour before Royce came back. He looked upset and more so when he saw her with Freddy, as he'd asked her to call him. Before Royce could say anything Freddy spoke up, his voice very strong and full of confidence. "You have yourself a very wonderful woman there, Hunter. You going to make an honest woman out of her?" Freddy smiled and held up his hand before Royce could answer. "Never mind. I'm an old man and I like to see people happy. If you'll come by my home sometime tomorrow, I'll have those papers signed for you. You should have sent her to me and this would have been over several days ago."

"All right. I'll do that. And she is something, isn't she? Thank you." Royce wrapped his arm around her again. "Is there anything you'd like to change in the contract? I realize now that we didn't give you a lot of options. And I wanted to tell you that your employees, they'll all be well taken care of."

"Thank you for that. And no, the contract is perfect the way it is. But I do have one favor. I'd like to buy Kasey here that piece in the other room. The blue raku thingy. Consider it a signing bonus if you will." Freddy leaned in and kissed her on the cheek. "That's for not letting me get by with it."

After he walked away she looked up at Royce. He looked…well, he looked pleased. When he started to guide her toward another room, she started trying to explain. "I didn't do anything. He came up to me. I don't…he was talking about how you were going to force him out of his business and… Where the hell are you taking me?"

They were just walking up to a door she'd never noticed on her first trip through this room. When he opened it and started to take her inside, she stopped him. He leaned down, took her earlobe into his mouth, and nipped. She felt her knees wobble.

"Either you go inside willingly or I throw you over my shoulder and take you in." He buried his face in her neck and gave her an open-mouthed kiss there. "Of course there is always option three."

Her panties soaked. She could feel the dampness of them and shifted so that she could try and alleviate some of the pressure she felt in her pussy. She'd gone from trying to explain something to him to needing him to touch her in a matter of seconds.

"And that would be what?" she asked him huskily.

He pressed his cock into her belly before he answered her. "I take you right here." She went with him.

The door barely closed when she was pressed up against it. His mouth was eating voraciously at hers. His tongue speared in her mouth, dueled with her own, and tortured her in ways she couldn't believe.

His hands were everywhere. He cupped her ass, bringing her flush against him. He was at her breasts, lifting them up and plucking at her nipples. When his hand slid up the slit in the side of her dress, she felt him growl low and her body flooded with need.

"How do I get you free?" he asked as he tugged at the top of her dress. "I want to suckle at your nipple, take it into my mouth."

She reached up and pulled the tiny eye hooks loose. The dress fit her so tightly all it did was open and drape at her breast. Royce peeled it from her slowly, kissing and laving her skin as he exposed it. When her breast was bared her nipple puckered tight and she felt herself swell with need. Royce took the hard tip into his mouth and worried it with his tongue before he began to suck.

"Royce," she shouted before she remembered the people on the other side of the door. "Please. Please, you're killing me."

"I need to be inside of you, Kasey," he said near her ear. "I want to take you right now, but I have to taste you. Your scent, Christ, woman, I can smell how aroused you are, and I'm nearly ready to burst."

He lowered himself to the floor, taking her dress down as he went. He pressed kisses and bites all the way down as he went to his knees. When she was standing before him with just her thigh-high stockings, panties, and shoes. She lifted her hands to cover herself. He stilled her with his hand.

"Don't. You're much too lovely and sexy to cover any part of you. I want to see you when I lick you. I want to see your face when I drink from you." He slid his hand up the inside of her thigh and he moaned. "You're so wet your thighs are soaked with your juices. Will you come when I lick you with my tongue?"

"Immediately. I ache, Royce. Please, help me." She wrapped her hand into his hair to bring him to her heat. "Please, you have to give me relief."

"Gladly," he said as he leaned in. When she felt her eyes flutter closed before he touched her, she opened them again when he told her to. She watched as he licked her thigh, nibbled at her hip bone, and touched her legs. When his hand ran up the back of her knee she trembled. When he kissed the top of her mound, she whimpered.

"Kasey, I don't want to marry ever. But for now, just until the baby is born, you're all mine," he commanded of her. "All mine. And so is this child. Mine."

He moved the scrap of lace away and suckled her clit into his mouth. Kasey put her hand over her mouth and screamed. Her climax was overwhelming. She felt as if an electrical wire had been touched to her skin. Molten lava felt as if it spread over her body and surged though her veins. Screaming out again when he entered her with his finger, she began riding the waves; over and over she rocked against his mouth and his fingers. Her fingers gripped his hair as a lifeline. She would have agreed to anything if he'd asked.

Her body was still jerking and riding the climax when he stood. She was too dazed in her own release to realize what he was doing. Her back was on the floor and he was between her legs. When he freed his cock, she reached for him, wanting to taste him as he'd done her.

"You touch me and I'm done. I need to be inside of you now. I don't know how long... Christ, Kasey, I'm ready to come just looking at you."

For all his urgency, he filled her slowly, softly almost. And when he was seated inside of her he leaned down and took her mouth. His kiss was hungry yet not demanding, hot but not consuming. He moved in and out of her as if he had all the time in the world, as if he was cherishing her. It was then that Kasey realized she was in love with him, in love with Royce Hunter.

His release brought her again. He rocked in her over and over until she nearly screamed again, her body so close to coming. When he settled over her then rolled to his back, taking her with him, she wiped at the tears. She didn't want him to ask her questions right now. She wasn't sure how she'd answer.

"We should get back," he said. "Will you come home with me tonight, Kasey? I'd like to make love to you in a proper bed."

"Yes. Tonight. I'll go home with you tonight." She pulled away to get dressed and he let her. For some reason she couldn't fathom that made her heart hurt.

CHAPTER 15

Annamarie watched the couple wander about the room. She smiled when Royce ran his hand down Kasey's back and nearly burst out laughing when the little chit smacked him and glared. The two of them were going to be a lot of fun to watch. She wondered how long it would be before either of them figured out that they were in love.

"They ever figure out what you did and they'll be really pissed at you, Mom." She turned to look at her son. "Do you think they're in love yet?"

"Yes. And Curtis Hunter, I have no idea what you're talking about. I did nothing at all to either of them. What a thing to say to your own mother."

He laughed. "Of course, how silly of me. You didn't tell Royce not to marry her because you really didn't want him to. And you didn't convince us that it was true as well. Mother," he said with mock sternness, "you try that on me, and I'll see you for the fraud you are."

She only smiled. She knew she already had someone picked out for him. Curtis hadn't been easy to match up. Well, for that matter, neither had the girl. If Curtis thought Kasey was a hard nut, wait until he... That was down the road. She wanted to see Royce married and happy first. She decided to change the subject.

"What have you found out about that White person? Is he still making noises about suing Kasey?" Annamarie smiled when she noticed Royce usher Kasey to a dark corner. She wondered if they'd make it home before they had to pull over to a dark street.

"Yes. He seems to think she was the reason he's being sued. There are now six other women that left because of his poor treatment. And so far only two of them aren't going to come forward." She glanced at him when he seemed to hesitate. "One of them claims he forced her into having sex with him that resulted in a child. She is willing to have a DNA test done next week."

That was unexpected. Annamarie knew about the other women. Curtis and Royce had been keeping her up on the issue from day one. She walked to another piece of pottery and saw them attach a small sold sign on the piece she'd wanted. Oh well, she'd call the artist and see if he had anything else similar to the large blue vase and buy it.

"There's this woman at the newspaper I want you to contact when this is over. She'll put a nice spin on it, if that's even possible. She knows what's happening, of course. I've been talking to her father. I want it out there that we are doing everything possible to make this right. Also,"—she looked at her son—"I want you to make sure that it never happens again. Never."

"It won't. I've already taken steps to make sure we're doing a better background check. There are also agencies that will help us with weeding out others like White. I've started a retraining program for our officers that we have and most, if not all, like the changes." He handed her a thick envelope. "This I did on my own. If things go the way I think they will with White we could have a major falling out. I've come up with a press release that I want you and Kasey to give. But you have to convince her to help you.'

She and Kasey still hadn't spoken. The girl avoided her at every turn. Annamarie looked at Curtis and frowned, but he was already shaking his head at her.

"She doesn't like me. This is a bad idea if you think that she and I could put our differences aside and make this work. I hurt her and she has every—"

"Maybe so. But you want her to be a part of our family then you have to figure out a way to make nice. And if they don't marry, and that is a good possibility, then I for one want to bounce the baby on my knee. It may be the only chance I get to do so."

Annamarie nodded. She thought he was wrong about them marrying, but didn't say anything. She took the envelope and put it in her handbag. With a deep breath she walked toward Kasey with Curtis close behind. She felt as if she were walking to her demise. Putting on a smile she knew would look strained, she kissed Royce on the cheek and looked at Kasey.

She nearly laughed when she saw a blush creep over Kasey's face. That's when she noticed that her hair wasn't quite as perfect and her dress was slightly wrinkled. Annamarie glanced at her son and noticed that his shirt was misbuttoned. She knew the exact moment when Kasey saw it too.

"Royce, darling," Annamarie started with a small laugh, "why don't you go and freshen up? You look a little…overdone. I'll keep an eye on Kasey while you're gone."

"Mom, I don't think that—"

"Royce, your shirt has lipstick on it and you've done it up incorrectly. Please, you know you don't want to make a bad impression on the patrons here. I promise to be nice to her. I'd like to...I need to tell her I'm sorry.'

As he walked away with Curtis, he turned back to look at them several times before he disappeared around the corner. Annamarie turned to Kasey when she started talking.

"I don't need your apology, Mrs. Hunter. I'm the one who was rude to you. I can see now that you were only protecting your son. I was only making a list. I'm a terrible list maker."

"It has been pointed out to me that I may have expected you to be impressed by me. Well, not so much me, but by my name and money. And to be honest, I did think that you should have been." Annamarie raised her hand when Kasey started to speak. "I did. I've been having people bowing and scraping at my feet for so long I just expected it."

Kasey snorted. "I don't impress easily, nor do I bow and scrape to anyone. And if you've come to expect that then there is no way you can be impressed by much. You seem like a woman who needs to get her hands dirty again."

Annamarie smiled. "I believe you're right. And you're going to help me. We need to blow this bastard White out of the water and help the other women like you...well, not like you. Women he'd taken advantage of and hurt. You, my dear, are much too stubborn and strong to have let him get you, aren't you?"

Kasey looked to where Royce had gone. Annamarie knew that look. It was of love and longing. When Kasey glanced back at her, Annamarie saw the sprinkle of tears in her eyes before she turned away.

"Have you told him, my dear?" Kasey looked at her when she asked. "You love him, don't you? I'm happy for you both. He is—"

"He doesn't want me. Just the child. He told me...he made it perfectly clear that he wants this baby, but he never... I'm a fool." Kasey fumbled for a tissue in her small handbag and wiped at the tears. "You won't tell him, will you? Please don't. It will only serve to make him pissed and he's that enough at me."

Annamarie wanted to pull the young woman into her arms and hold her. She also wanted to go and find her son and beat his ass.

"I won't tell him, I promise. But I think you're wrong, Kasey. I think he loves you as much as you do him." Kasey stiffened and Annamarie knew her son was returning. "If you ever need to talk, you can call me."

Kasey nodded, but somehow, she knew she'd never hear from her. The girl was just as stubborn as her son and she wanted to scream at both of them. But she simply accepted the kiss from Royce and watched as they walked away.

~~~

Kasey came home with Royce. He could see that she was slightly overwhelmed by the house. Hell, he was too, but he was beginning to like the big place. The construction on the second floor was nearly complete and he'd moved all his things into the large office just today. He took Kasey to the kitchen.

"Are you hungry? I had groceries delivered today. The housekeeper put it all away, but I'm sure there are things I'm still missing. I doubt I'll ever fill the pantry. It's as big as someone's small apartment. But I like it." He realized he was babbling. He took a deep breath and began to pull out the fixings for a couple of sandwiches. "I could cook you something if you'd like."

"No. Whatever you're having is fine. I'm not really very hungry." She moved to the sink and washed her hands. "What can I do to help you?"

Her voice sounded sad. He didn't know what had happened between her and his mother, but he knew it wasn't bad. Not in the sense that they were still angry with each other. His mother had been acting strangely too after he'd come back, he only just realized. Kasey wasn't her usual smart-assed self. And he realized that he missed it. He decided that he'd risk pissing her off just to get her fired up again.

"I thought maybe I'd move you in here." He grinned to himself when she stiffened. "That way I can make sure you're eating properly. Then there is your employment. I think you need to stop working until the baby is born. That way if—"

"Stop working," she said in a low growl. "I most certainly will not quit working, you egoistical asshole. And I'm not moving in this monster. It would take a week just to clean it. And—"

"I'd hire you some staff. You'd not have to lift a finger. As for the name calling, that'll have to—" His head snapped back. He didn't know which of them was more surprised by her punch to his nose, her or him. He grabbed the towel off the counter when he felt the blood seep down his chin and glared at her. He hadn't meant to make her that mad. But looking at her, he swallowed whatever he was about to say.

She was crying. Great sobbing sounds came from her and tears streamed down her face. When he stepped toward her to hold her, she took three steps back and nearly tripped over the chair. He stopped. He didn't want her hurt; he'd already done that enough.

"Kasey, honey, I was—"

"I hit you. I didn't...I shouldn't have hit you. No matter how mad you make me, I know that violence isn't the answer." She sat down then popped back up. "I need to go home. I need to...you can't believe how sorry I am that I...please, I need to go home. I'll call a cab."

"Kasey, honey, please don't leave. I was trying to make you angry. Something had made you up—"

"You wanted me mad at you?" she asked incredulously. "You baited me until...are you insane? Of course you are. What sane person would piss someone off on purpose? I can't believe...well, I don't have a clue why I didn't believe it. Look at your track record so far. You people seem to thrive on pissing people off."

"Now just a minute. I told you I was—"

"No," she snapped back. "I don't care what your reasons are. Do you have any idea how emotional I am right now? I feel like everything anyone says to me makes me want to burst into tears. That man tonight, the one that bought me that vase, do you know that he treated me better than you did just now and he was a stranger? You wanted to make me mad. Well I hope you're fucking happy because you—"

He kissed her. Probably not the smartest move to get that close to a pissed off hormonal woman, but he wanted to touch her. Needed to hold her. And he was willing to have some of his parts bruised to do so.

Her body softened by degrees. Her mouth was firm beneath his, but she didn't fight too hard to get away. He wanted to feel her wrapped around him, her body touching his, so he lifted her against him, sat her on the counter, and stepped between her legs. He pulled away long enough to look down at her, but didn't back away.

"You are so beautiful when you're pissed," he told her softly. "I love the way your eyes spark daggers and your arms move. Your breasts do the most amazing dance when you do that." He cupped one gently as he leaned down to run his tongue over the top. "And the way you look when you come makes my cock hard just thinking about it."

"Stop it," she told him as she arched into his body. "I'm mad at you. How could you do that to me? I realize that you only want the baby, but you could be a lot nicer to me until you have it."

Royce felt as if she'd hit him. It wasn't so much what she said, but that she would believe that he only wanted the baby. He took another step back when something else occurred to him. "I love you."

CHAPTER 16

Kasey was standing in her kitchen when the phone rang again. She'd not answered it all afternoon and she wasn't planning on it now. She knew it was her uncle; he wanted to know what the doctor said. Well, she wasn't ready to talk to anyone just yet.

Royce had taken her home that night after he'd told her he loved her. She remembered thinking her heart was going to explode with happiness when just as suddenly as he'd said it, he told her he couldn't be in love with her. It felt as if he'd broken it. She glanced at the papers on the table and then walked to the refrigerator to get something to drink. She couldn't look at it or the check that was lying there that Curtis had given her before he'd left.

"I think my brother is an ass if you want to know the truth." She'd looked over at him. He'd taken her to the doctor as he said he would and had brought her home after.

"You shouldn't be mad at your brother, Curtis. You never know what might happen and you'd never be able to live with yourself if you were mad at him like this and something horrible happened. What's between us...what's happening between us is only temporary. I told you what I wanted."

"I think that's a mistake as well. Kasey, please let me talk to him before you do something stupid."

She wasn't being stupid. She was being smart for the very first time in all her life. She was giving Royce just what he wanted. His child. She sat at the table and picked up the papers. They said that the money was hers to use as she saw fit and that all she needed to do was to give the child his name and put his name as the father on the birth certificate.

Picking up the pen with shaky fingers, she signed her name and dated it then she promptly burst into tears. Falling in love shouldn't hurt this badly. She signed the check and then before she changed her mind, she put it all in the next day air envelope and picked up her phone. She noticed there were seven messages there, but ignored them. She called the courier service and made arrangements for them to pick up her package then called her uncle.

"I've been worried about you. What happened? Is everything all right?"

She gave a wavering smile. "Yes. I'm pregnant. I have a due date of February fourteenth. Everything looks fine. The baby is small, but he said that would change. He told me it was too early to tell the sex, but I told him I didn't care. How are you?"

He was quiet for a long time before he spoke. "Now that you've gotten that out of your system, tell me what's really going on."

She nearly lied to him again. It wouldn't have been easy, but she knew that starting a conversation with, "I'm giving up the baby" wouldn't be the best thing for her right now. But she knew that she had to. If nothing else then to give him time to get used to the idea.

"I've come to some decisions. Major ones that involve my future. Things that—"

"Just tell me, girl. You're killing me. What is wrong? Is it the baby or is it you?" She heard him take a deep breath before he continued. "You've decided to get an abortion, haven't you?"

She felt the tears fall. "No, not an abortion. I couldn't do that. But I can't keep it. I've...I'm giving it up. It's better that way."

She waited for him to explode. But he didn't. He was calm and rational, something she needed and actually should have expected from him.

"You're the one that has to live with your decision either way. I can't say I'm not disappointed, because I am. I think you'd make a terrific mom; you're too much like your mom not to. But I can also see why you'd feel the need to do this." He sighed again. "Honey, what does Royce think about this?"

Now came the hardest part. She needed her uncle to trust her more than anyone she knew. Trust her with her secret.

"I'm signing the baby over to him as soon as it's born. He doesn't know. He...I need him not to know until it's done. You have to trust me on this."

"May I at least ask you why?"

She wiped at the tears as she formed her answer. "He can give the baby the best. Something that I can't do, like education, opportunities, and everything that it will need."

"You didn't."

Those two softly spoken words crushed her. She knew he wasn't saying it, but it made her feel like a failure—like somehow, she'd failed not only her child but her family as well. She couldn't answer him. She hurt so badly that she simply hung up the phone.

The courier came ten minutes later and after he left to take the envelope to Curtis, she laid down. It was early yet, not quite six o'clock, but she felt as if she'd been run through a gauntlet. She was asleep as soon as her head hit the pillow.

When she woke around two in the morning she felt sick. Her body ached and her head was pounding. Moving to the kitchen she put on her tea kettle and, while it was set to boil, she got down her mug. The pain ripped through her like a knife. The next pain knocked her to her knees. That's when she noticed the blood.

She reached for the phone, knocking it off the table and onto the floor beside her. She reached for it, the pain making her scream out again. Pressing what she hoped was the number two, she prayed for her uncle to answer before the pain took her away. Even as someone answered, she felt her body let go. The blood poured from her as she said help.

~~~

Royce rushed to the hospital, not even aware if he stopped at any of the lights on the way. Daniel had said she was hurt and that the doctors wouldn't tell him anything. Royce remembered asking about her uncle and was assured he was on his way as well. Royce rushed in the emergency room and right into Jay York's arms.

"Where is she? Is she all right?" He realized that Jay was speaking to him but couldn't seem to understand. "Just tell me she's all right."

"They took her to surgery. She was awake when I saw her briefly, but she… There was…oh God, there was so much blood. All I could think about was her mom. I saw Leah all over again."

Royce held the man as he cried. Blood, Royce thought, so much blood. He wondered if it was an aneurism and tried to shy his mind from that. But he knew she'd lost the baby, lost their child.

"She didn't lose the baby," Jay said before he could ask. "She...the doctor said that she was lucky and that she'd have to stay down for a bit, but there was a good chance that she'd deliver to term. She was so scared and crying. She said to tell you she didn't do anything to hurt the baby. She wanted you to know that she'd never do anything like that, ever. I didn't...she'll be all right, he said. He said she'd be just fine."

Royce looked at him. Why would... "I never thought she did. Why would she think something like that? Why would she have you tell me something like that?"

"Because she had it in her head that all you wanted was the kid." Royce turned to his brother Daniel as he spoke. "She talked to Curtis today. Everything was set up that you'd get custody of the baby once it was born. The money you sent to her last week was going into a trust fund for her aunt's care. And then once she left the hospital she was leaving the area."

Royce sat down in one of the plastic chairs, feeling as though someone had hit him. He rubbed his chest where most of the pain radiated from. She believed that. He knew he had given her no reason to believe otherwise, but it hurt him to know that he'd hurt her.

"The doctor, did he say what happened? Did he know why she'd lost so much blood?" Jay was shaking his head. "Then what happened to them?"

"He said that she'd been slightly underweight anyway and her body was telling her that she needed to take it easy. He said these things just happen and that she was one of the lucky ones. After a few days in here, she can go home with me then I'll—"

Royce saw his mother come through the doors. He needed her. Needed to have his mother tell him that things were going to be all right. He stood up when she came toward him. Between the three of them, she was brought up to speed and they went up to the surgery floor.

The doctor had closed off the small tear in her womb, but it would be hours yet before they would be sure that everything was fine. Two hours later they were all sitting in her room. Jay had cleared it with the hospital that they could be there. Royce had already told them that he was staying until she left or threw him out. He was reasonably sure that he could very well be thrown out, but he was willing to take the chance. He looked up when Kasey made a small noise.

She looked right at him. He could see the pain in her eyes and he hurt for her. He moved his chair closer to the bed and took her hand. He kissed it gently and smiled at her.

"The doctor said you're going to be fine. That you might be weak for a few days, but otherwise, you'd be all right." She nodded. "Do you need anything? Food? Something to drink?"

"No." She looked over at the people behind him then back at him. "Why are you here?"

"Daniel called me when you called him. He thinks you might have hit last called when you picked up the phone. He said you kept calling for your uncle."

"I don't remember that. I was...I was hurting and I thought I'd dialed Uncle Jay. I'm sorry I bothered him." She turned her head and wiped at the tear with her other hand. "I lost the baby. Your baby. I'm sorry about that. You don't need to hang around now. I'll understand if you—"

"No, Kasey, you didn't. It was close, the doctor said, but you didn't lose him. You'll need to be on bed rest for a while, but that...Kasey, I love you. I'm sorry for the way I've been—"

"Don't please. It's not important anymore. It's okay that you don't love me. The baby made you—"

He put his hand over her mouth gently. "Don't tell me that I don't love you. It's taken me nearly thirty years to figure out that I do and I plan to say it a great deal. So unless you have something profound to say back to me then I want you to hush and get better."

She looked over his shoulder as he felt someone coming near. He thought it was her uncle and moved out of his way so that he could see his niece. Royce didn't let go of her hand and stayed close enough that he could see her. Royce didn't want to be rude, but the thought of leaving her right now was something he didn't want to think about. When Jay kissed her forehead and moved back Royce slid his chair back in front of her.

"You should go home. There is no reason for you to hang around here. I'm really...I'm really tired anyway." Her voice broke as she spoke and he brushed her tears away with his thumb. "Royce, please."

"I'm not leaving you, honey. I do love you and I want to be here with you. Short of you kicking me out, I'll just sit outside at the nurse's station, but I'm not leaving." She turned her head and he pulled it back to face him. "I love you, Kasey Marie York. The sooner you get used to hearing me say that, the better off you'll be."

CHAPTER 17

Kasey went home four days later. There was really no reason for her to have stayed the extra day, but Royce had insisted and the staff, whether charmed or bullied by him, had done as he'd asked. She didn't care. She just simply didn't care. It was where they'd taken her that pissed her off.

"I can very well stay on my own or with my uncle. In fact, I'd rather stay with him. Take me there. I have absolutely no reason to stay with you." She'd said this same thing a total of eight times now and she knew she was wasting her breath. "I insist that you listen to me and take me back to my apartment this minute."

"You're very cute when you get all bossy," Royce told her with a cocky grin. "But your uncle agrees that you shouldn't be left alone. I'm taking a few days off and I'll be caring for you. It'll be fun."

Fine, she thought, let him care for her all he wanted, but she wasn't speaking to him. See how he liked being frustrated. She turned in the seat of his monster car and looked out the window. She just wanted to have some quiet time. She'd been denied that for the past few days and she wanted it.

She'd nearly lost her baby. She'd been so very lucky, the doctor told her, and then he'd explained what she needed to do to keep the baby and to stay healthy. She just needed to take it easy, avoid stress, and make sure that she didn't lift anything more than ten pounds until the little guy was born. And he told her she was having a boy. She looked up when the car stopped.

The house was magnificent. Tall pillars of white graced the front of the long, open porch. There was a beautiful lace-worked railing surrounding it and she could see that someone had set several rockers around it in varying colors. The large urns were filled with bright flowers that spilled over and the floor to roof windows sparkled in the morning light. The brick façade was rich in deep-colored clay and the grout was creamy against each one. She was startled when someone picked her up out of the car and started to carry her.

"Put me down, you moron. I can walk. I was told to walk, as a matter of fact." So much for not speaking to him, she thought. Maybe she'd just yell, that would certainly piss—

He kissed her mouth and all thoughts just flew away.

"I'm carrying you because I want to. Now hush up. I want you to take a nap. The doctor said that you'd need to rest as much as possible these first few days and you're not to lift anything over—"

"I'm very aware what the doctor said. Even though you tried your best to make me seem like a simpleton, I heard and actually understood every word he said." He grinned at her as he set her on the porch. "I want you to take me to my uncle's house if you won't let me go home. This is ridiculous for you to miss work for me."

"No," he said as he unlocked the door. When the door opened, he scooped her up again and took her inside. When he set her down, she turned to look around. There were several people standing there looking at them when they entered. "I want you to meet the staff. I've been very lucky in that I was able to get someone so quickly to help us out. This is Mrs. Apple. She does the cooking when I'm not in the mood. This is Mrs. Jankins. She helps out around the house and she—"

"May I have a word with you?" She had to tell him that enough was enough. And as much as she wanted to scream at him again, she wouldn't do it in front of the people who worked for him. She'd had that done to her enough to know how embarrassing it was. He picked her up again and she squealed.

"I'll just take Miss York up to our room. If you wouldn't mind fixing her a tray...what would you like, Kasey? They can—"

She leaned into his ear and bit him. Hard. "I want you to fucking put me down and stop carting me around like a bab—" The tears came hot and fast. She buried her face in his neck and didn't say another word. She knew that he'd carried her up the stairs. She knew that he'd spoken to the two ladies there in the hall and the two others she'd not learned the names of. She wanted to crawl in a hole and simply lay there. The bed beneath her made her roll into a ball and weep.

She didn't know how long it was before she fell asleep, but she woke to a semi-dark room and a warm, hard body next to her. She tried to roll away from him, knowing that it was Royce, but he pulled her back and snuggled over her breast.

Kasey lay there, her heart pounding and her body needing his. She tried again to pull away, to get up to use the bathroom, but wasn't able to budge him.

"Royce, let me up. I have to use the bathroom." He groaned when she punched his arm. "Royce, let go of me. I have to pee."

He rolled and let her go, but before she could get the blanket off and stand, he was there. She wanted to tell him she was fine, but the room tilted a bit and she had to grab onto him or fall. He held her up, speaking to her in low, soothing tones. She laid her forehead on his chest.

"I have to pee." She hated the way her voice sounded small and weak. "I just…I think I'm fine now. If you'll just tell me where my clothes are, I'd like to take a shower too."

"I don't think so. Not unless you take one with me. Come on, I'll help you to the bathroom and then we'll get you changed." He held her close, but he didn't pick her up this time.

"I feel fine. I promise to take a quick one. And I won't lock the door." He laughed, but said nothing. "Seriously, Royce, this is stupid. I want to…I need to take a shower. I feel nasty."

He stopped walking and she looked at him. He looked so…sad, and her heart thudded in her chest. Before she could tell him that she was sorry that she was being a pain in the ass, he kissed her gently on the mouth. Then he leaned his forehead to hers.

"I don't…I can't tell you how I felt when my brother called me. He was hysterical with worry that I nearly didn't know what he was saying. He said you were screaming for your uncle. That you kept telling him that there was so much blood. He'd thought…he told me later that all he could think about was that someone had broken in and that they had hurt you. I couldn't breathe for not knowing. I got a ticket on my way to the hospital." He kissed her again before continuing. "I love you, Kasey. I know you find that hard to believe after what I've done to you, said to you, but I do. I love you so very much."

He took her the rest of the way to the bathroom and she let him. She didn't fuss at him when he insisted on helping her with the toothpaste, nor did she say anything when he turned the shower on. She did, however, speak up when he started to peel off his own clothes.

"I'm not taking a shower with you," she told him as she gripped her own T-shirt over her hips. "I can't. You have to...Royce, please don't. I'm...I've had...I'm not ready for this. The doctor said no sex so I can't take a shower with you."

He stopped undressing and stared at her before he nodded. "Kasey, I'm not an animal. Having sex with you...well, I was going to say is the last thing on my mind, but that would be a lie. I want you with all my heart. But I'm still going to get in with you. You take care of whatever it is you need to for five minutes then I'll get in and clean up too. I won't...I won't touch you unless you need me too, but honey, I'm just as nasty-feeling. I've not had even a sponge bath in three days and I need a shower too."

She supposed she could have insisted that he take one after her, but she only nodded. Kasey turned her back on him while he brushed his own teeth and she hurried into the shower. She wanted to be clean in the worst way possible. She ducked her head under the shower to get her hair wet again when she heard the door open behind her.

Kasey had never had anyone wash her hair for her before. She thought maybe her mom had done it for her as a child, but no one since she'd become an adult. When Royce took the shampoo from her and started massaging it into her hair, she nearly moaned. When he told her to stand under the spray and rinse, she felt his cock brush slightly against her hip. She froze.

~~~

Royce wanted her. He wanted her in ways he didn't understand yet, but was very happy to explore with her. But more than anything, he wanted to simply hold her. She was his world right now and he wanted her to realize that.

He knew that she'd felt his cock. He'd have to be a dead man not to want her. He wouldn't hurt her, wouldn't even touch her because he didn't want to hurt her. He pulled her to his chest and held her to him.

"Royce, I can't—"

"I know. I just want to hold you. I'm sorry if I make you feel uncomfortable like this, but Christ, woman, you're beautiful and sexy to me." She shook her head and he brought her mouth to his for a quick kiss. "I know sexy when I see it and you are so. Now, let's get cleaned up so you can get back to bed. I can feel you getting a little shaky."

The shower wasn't what he'd hoped for when he'd thought of getting naked with her like this. He helped her wash her back and she returned the favor. By the time he got out, he was in pain, but he didn't say anything. He wanted her to know that he wanted her in his life, not only his bed. He gave her one more of his shirts, put her into his bed, and she fell asleep within a few minutes. He kissed her on the forehead and after getting dressed himself, he left her to her quiet to call his mom.

"She'll be fine, Royce. She just needs to rest and take it easy. It can't be easy for her right now. Poor thing has lost so much."

He felt tears gather in his eyes when he thought of the amount he'd taken from her all on his own. "She hasn't said she loves me. I wonder...do you think she ever will?" He wished he knew, wished he knew that she could forgive him. "She cried again."

He heard his mother laugh softly. "She will be doing that a lot for the next few weeks. The doctor said her body will have hormonal rushes because she's pregnant. And honey, crying is the least of your problems. She's going to be an emotional bouncing ball."

"I want her to be mad at me again. Hell, I'd take her throwing something at me rather than tears. They hurt more than her punches do." He smiled. If Kasey heard him say that, she'd probably make him regret it. "And she's not eating much. She needs to stay healthy and she won't be able to do that eating like a bird. I had Margo bake up some sweet stuff to tempt her."

"You should call her uncle. I'm sure Jay knows something she really likes. Also Bobbie. Bobbie is sweet on Jay and I'm betting she knows more about that family than anyone." He heard her say something then come back on the line. "Donald said to tempt her with a shopping spree. He said his wife will do most anything for that. And no, I did not ask him what she'd do. I believe that goes under the heading of too much information."

Royce started to laugh. His mother was one of a kind. He did think about the shopping trip, though. She would need some clothes while she was recuperating. While he enjoyed her wearing his shirts, he wondered how practical that would be once she was up and about. He made a mental note to see about getting one of the local stores to gather some things up and bring them to her. He wondered how he'd figure out sizes when his mother spoke again.

"Now about her living there. You know I don't really like it so you'll either have to make more permanent arrangements with her or send her to her uncle's. I'd actually prefer that you marry her. I like her a great deal and your brothers can't say enough good things about her. But as before, I don't think you should. You can't possible think that—"

"If she'll have me after this, I want to marry her. I'm in love with her." She didn't say anything for several seconds. "I am in love with her. I think I have been for some time. She certainly has no reason to love me, but I'm going to work on that."

He realized then that he really did want her to love him. He'd been fighting with her and mostly himself for so long that he'd fallen in love with the most wonderful woman in the world. And he'd been a complete ass the entire time too.

"I should have shut up and listened to you all. But...Mom, you had it so great with Dad that I didn't want to lose her, I think. I know what it did to you to have Dad die like he did and I didn't...I'm an idiot."

"Yes, you are. But you've finally come to your senses and have finally admitted that you're going to love her no matter what. And, Royce, you should know that she loves you too. I think she has for some time." He heard her clear her throat. "Do you have any idea how happy I am for you?"

"No...yes. I'm happy too. And I want her to love me, but I'm afraid that it's going to take me some time to convince her of that."

"Good. Then you'll need to work faster. You're not getting any younger and the thought of having a grandbaby just makes me all simple in the head. But don't you dare rush her." He laughed at his mom before she continued. "Also, let's try very hard not to piss her off too much this time, son. And don't think I've forgotten that you didn't practice safe sex with her and that's how you got yourself in the situation you're in now."

"Yes, ma'am. I know. And if she'll let me knock her up every year for the next twenty, then who am I to turn a lovely lady down? And just for the record, I know there were only six months between your marriage and my birth." He disconnected the call with his mother sputtering. He figured he was going to pay for that, but for now he'd live with it. His next call was to Jay. It just so happened that Bobbie was there too.

KATHI S. BARTON

CHAPTER 18

Jay watched his niece come toward him. She'd been at Royce's house for over three weeks and she had called him this morning and asked him to come and get her. He wasn't sure what to do so he'd called Mr. Royce at work. The man had been positively livid when he'd found out.

"Hold her…well, try. If nothing else, I want you to stall her. I can be there in twenty minutes." Jay started to tell him that he would when Mr. Royce spoke again. "I won't hurt her, but there are times when I want to beat her butt. Damned girl."

Jay knew just how the man felt. There were days when he wanted to beat her himself. Just like he had with her mother. But this woman was much more independent than her mother had ever been. Scarily so.

"Are you ready to go?" she asked as she pulled on her jacket. "Royce is at work today and I don't know how much time I have before he comes home. And I need to get back to my own place. This is…Uncle Jay?"

"He's coming now. I thought he'd…he's on his way here and should be here soon. I'm sorry, baby, but the man loves you and I don't want you to be alone." She sat down in the chair and stared at him. "He said he loves you. Don't you believe him?"

"I don't...I don't want him to love me. I mean, yes, I know he does, or at least he says he does, but Uncle Jay, he's so out of my league. We are as different as night and day. He has so much and I'm lucky to have a pot to piddle in."

"What a really stupid thing to say." She opened her mouth to say something, but he raised his hand. "No, you listen to me, young lady. Do you think that a couple comes together with the exact same things? No, they do not. You think your aunt and I had even close to the same desires or...you know, that's a bad reference. I hated your aunt. Yes, I know that's hard to believe, but it wasn't until later after—"

"I know you hated her. We all did for what she did to Suzy. But this isn't the same. Royce doesn't treat me like that. He treats me with respect and understanding. I just..."

"You just what?" Royce asked from the doorway. "You just what, Kasey? I'd really like to know because I do love you. I'm going to love you for the rest of our lives whether you care for me or not."

Jay watched her. He needed more than anything to see if she loved him. He did feel badly for calling Mr. Royce when he should have sided with her, but he knew that Leah would have skinned him alive had he just taken Kasey home with him without seeing for himself. He watched the young man walk slowly toward Kasey and drop to one knee before her. Jay knew he'd made the right decision when he saw Kasey's eyes light up when he touched her.

Jay thought he should leave them to their privacy, but Bobbie told him if he didn't come back with details she'd never forgive him. He smiled at that. Who would have thought that little Bobbie would be such a passionate little thing? And her in love with him too. Jay decided that he'd been alone long enough and on his way home he was stopping to get a ring. Time to make things right for everyone.

Jay nearly fell off his chair when he saw Mr. Royce pull out a small blue box from his pocket. Then he got up quietly and left the room. Bobbie was going to have kittens. He was pulling out his cell phone to call her as he opened the front door. "You're not going to believe it," he said with a huge smile. "My Kasey is going to marry Mr. Royce."

~~~

"I don't want you to leave me. Please don't. I've...I love you. I know you're probably sick of hearing—"

"No, I'm not. It's just that...why?" He was startled by her question so much so that he was speechless. "I mean, if this is because you have some sense of obligation about the fact that I'm having your baby then you can just forget it. I don't need you. I have enough guilt of my own. I certainly don't need you to heap more onto me. And if you think I'm having sex with you again, then you can forget that too. I didn't particularly think you were all that good anyway."

He took her mouth. There was no finesse or even any kind of gentleness in his kiss, but she was breathless when he pulled back. Royce scooped her off the chair and into his arms. They were on the floor before she said a word and he simply silenced her with another kiss. He felt her wrap her legs around his hips as he moved his mouth along her neck.

He knew he'd have to be slow. The doctor had told them that she'd only be ready for sex when she was ready. When he'd talked to him again yesterday after her appointment, Royce had been told that she'd healed much better than he'd thought she would and that she had put on eight much needed pounds. Royce knew that the bleeding had stopped too. She'd told him that several weeks ago one morning.

He nuzzled her breast. He could feel the peaked tip beneath her bra and wanted to take it into his mouth. Her moan made him rock into her. Lifting her blouse, he ran his thumb up and under her bra and felt the heavy flesh as it tightened. He needed to taste her and moved the tiny scrap of lace out of his way and suckled her hard.

"Royce." She shouted his name as he moved to the other breast to give it its due. He was rolling her nipple on the roof of his mouth when her legs tightened around him. He wanted her needy; he wanted her to want him so badly that she'd beg him. He moved down her body and laved his tongue into her navel as she arched up into his cock.

He opened the snap on her jeans. And was rewarded with her fingers tangling in his hair, gripping him tightly against her. As her pants slid down over her hips he nipped and tasted her skin, feasted on her flesh, and delighted in the way she made him feel. He hoped that his plan didn't backfire and he was begging her, but he was going to give it his damnedest.

When he had her pants down around her thighs, her scant panties still in place, he sat up, pulled away from her heat and her scent. He pulled his shirt up and over his head and tossed it away. She lay before him like a bounty and he planned to gorge himself on her, but first, he needed to have her say yes.

"Marry me," he demanded of her as he ran his finger against her soaked panties. "Marry me and I'll let you come."

"What?" Her eyes were hazed and filled with lust and need. He wanted to tell her that he'd give her anything she wanted if only she'd look like that all the time, but he wanted her as his wife.

"I love you. Marry me I'll make you happy for the rest of our lives. Please." He begged her now as he slid his finger beneath her panties and deep into her. "Marry me, Kasey."

She moaned as she rode his finger. He watched her eyes flutter closed as she lifted her hands to her bare breasts. He was going to come before her if she kept that up so he stopped moving inside of her and watched as she opened her eyes.

"Royce, please. I'm so close. I need to come, please?" Her voice was low, seductive, and nearly a growl. He felt his cock leak in his pants. "Please?"

He slid his finger deep and stopped again. He watched her try and move against him and he pulled back. He was dying. Her scent, her musk was heady and strong. He found himself leaning forward to drink from her and just barely managed to hold himself steady. Royce moved his finger again, slowly.

"You know what I want. If you tell me yes, I'll give you want you need." She sat up and pulled his mouth to hers. He had to pull away or he'd have her regardless of her answer. "Marry me."

He reached for the box he'd dropped to the floor when he'd first knelt before her. Opening the small box he watched as her eyes widened in surprise and then she looked at him with tears in her eyes.

"You mean it? You really want to marry me?"

He nodded, not sure if he could speak for his breath caught in his throat.

"You're going to regret this; you know that, don't you? I'm not going to change and I'm certainly not going to give into you like this again."

"Okay. I can live with that so long as you're mine." He waited for more and when she didn't give him an answer, he had to ask. "Is that a yes?"

"I want you to give me more children. Soon. I want...I would like lots of babies with you. Are you okay with that?"

He was nodding as he pulled the ring from the box. "And there will be no more ordering me about like I'm a simpleton. And I'm going to work for your brothers. *They* treat me with respect."

The ring slid onto her finger like he knew it would. He waited half a heartbeat before he put in a few of his own demands. "I want a good half dozen children and I expect you to raise them to be just like you. And as for working for my brothers." He kissed her, taking her tongue into his mouth as he slid his own along her deep heat. "They work for me so you'll be working for me too. And honey, I plan to show you how much I respect you right now."

He pressed against her clit as he moved his finger in and out of her. Her hands slid up over his shoulders as she kissed him again. As her arms wrapped around him he lowered her to the floor and then pulled back. Her whimper nearly had him do the same. She watched him as he stripped out of his pants and boxer briefs and wrapped his hand around his thick cock. He looked down at her.

"I want to come on you like this. I want to watch as my cum sprays all over you and see you come from it. Would you like that?" He moaned when she nodded at him and licked her lips. "You keep that up and there will be no choice in the matter."

"What if I wanted both from you? What if I wanted you to come on me then fuck me? Could you do that, Royce? Could you satisfy me twice in one night?" She moaned when he rubbed his cock at her entrance.

He pressed the head of his cock into her and stilled. His entire body tightened as she lifted her hips off the floor and rode him. Dizzy and so close to coming, he slid into her as he lifted her hips up off the floor then her entire body as he rested on his knees.

"Do you have any idea what you do to me? How you make my body ache for yours even when I'm not anywhere near you?" She wrapped her arms around his neck and took his mouth. Lifting her ass up over his cock, she threw back her head.

"Royce," she called out. "Please, Royce, I love you."

His world tilted on its axis. There was nothing but the two of them, no one around for miles, and nothing between them. Laying her back on the floor he settled between her thighs and her ankles wrapped around him.

"Say it again."

She looked at him, confused.

"Tell me that you love me again, Kasey. Say the words to me while I make love to you."

Kasey kissed him. It was tender and so sweet. Her lips didn't part for him and he was fine with it. When she tilted her head and stared up at him, he was sure she was going to tell him she'd made a mistake.

"I've never given my heart to anyone before. I've never…I didn't think I'd ever meet anyone where I would want to." She kissed him gently again. "I was positive it wasn't you too. But you saved me, didn't you? You kept me from being lonely and sad. I love you, Royce Hunter, and I do it with all my heart."

CHAPTER 19

Gilbert watched his only daughter. She was moving about the street like she fucking owned it. He sneered at the car that pulled up in front of the little store she was coming out of, but stood up straighter when the driver got out and helped her in it. When the hell had she been elevated up to limo status? When the car pulled away he stood watching it for several minutes after it was out of sight.

She was hooking was all he could figure. Found herself some rich dude and now she was living the high life. He wondered what her mother would say and realized he had no idea what Leah would have said. Hell, she'd probably been the one to set her kid up so'ins she'd have a nice ride after she was dead.

Gilbert wasn't happy about the turn of events on that either. He knew there'd been an insurance policy. That stupid one, Leah's sister, had told him that she was going to get her little sister's watch when she died. It wasn't until later when he'd seen Suzy at the old people's home that he realized she'd been talking about a policy. He'd gone to see the girl once a month after that just so's he'd get some information about them. The idiot had been a fountain of news until last week.

"I'm sorry, Mr. Gilbert, but Suzan has been taken to another home. She won't be coming here any longer as she and her brother have moved further away." Gilbert nodded, not having a clue what the nurse was yammering about. "The facilities can only take on people of Suzan's needs when they live within the district, and her family can afford more care for her now."

Now he knew why. That fucking brother of Leah's was making Gilbert's own daughter hook for him. And he wasn't even thinking of sharing in the profits. Gilbert crossed the street and nearly got hit for his trouble. He screamed at the driver to take a care—"veteran walking here"—as he moved to the sidewalk.

"Some people should have better respect for the men who gave up so much for our freedom." Gilbert turned to look at the person who spoke. "What tour were you in? I'm guessing Desert Storm?"

Gilbert hadn't a clue what this fucker was talking about either. Desert what? He pushed him away from him only just then realizing what he'd been saying. Gilbert threw back his head and laughed. He'd never been in the Army or any other part of the service either. Pansies. All of 'em, just plain old pansies.

Gilbert pulled out his cell phone and had dialed his daughter's number four times before he figured out his phone wasn't working. When he took the battery out twice and tried turning it on, he ended up tossing it into the trash. He just knew it was a conspiracy against him. No one ever helped out anyone anymore.

He thought about flagging down a taxi to get him home, but he didn't have any cash on him. Grinning, he realized he didn't ever have any cash on him, but that hadn't ever stopped him before. It took him twenty minutes to get there, stealing a few apples, a bag of chips, and three beers from the various stores he passed on the way. A brother had to eat and he thought he should have it all for free.

There was a pay phone in the lobby of the dump he lived in. It rarely worked and when it did, he usually didn't have the money to make the call. Today he'd been able to get himself a wallet and a ladies purse along with his lunch so he was flush for the minute. Sitting inside the dirty thing, he dialed Kasey's number and glared at no one in particular when she answered with a growl.

"What the hell do you want now? I've told you several times that I have no money to give you and even if I did, I wouldn't. Stop cal—"

"You'll have more respect for your daddy. I'm all you got left. And I don't believe you about the—"

He hated to be cut off when he had something to say and Kasey did it every time she said something to him. He was frankly getting sick of it and when she took a breath from her tirade, he was going to tell her so. But she said something that made him stop to listen.

"…married in a few weeks and you are so not welcome in that life either. I don't know where you get off thinking you are going to get daddy of the year from me, but you couldn't be further from the truth. I don't want you around me or my family."

"I am your family, damn it, and it's high time you started acting like it." Before she could tell him something again, he went on. "And what the fuck do you mean you're a getting married? You ain't had no man ask me for your hand. What the hell is that—"

Her shrill laughter broke him off. Of all the nerve of her, he thought. If she was here right now, he'd whoop her ass for her and then he'd—

Gilbert wasn't really sure what a man could do to his grown daughter, but didn't say anything as she continued to laugh.

"You might want to stay away from my future husband, daddy dearest. I'm pretty sure he'll knock you on your lazy ass as soon as you open your mouth about 'whooping' my ass." She took a deep breath. He could almost see her building up some steam to have another go. "You are not anything to me. As far as I'm concerned, you are nothing to me."

"Now see here, you can't go talking—"

"I want you out of my life, Gilbert. And I mean forever this time. I only let you come around out of respect for mom, but that ends now."

The phone went dead and he sat there staring at if for a full five minutes before he hung it up. He staggered his way to the stairs—the elevator never worked anyway—and went down the hall to his room.

"Girl oughta have more respect for the man that sired her," he mumbled to himself. "What's this world comin' to when a kid thinks they can get off talking—"

"Mr. MacDonald, Gilbert MacDonald?" Gilbert looked at the man standing there in his fancy suit and briefcase. "Are you Gilbert MacDonald?"

"Tell me what you want him for and I'll let you know if'n it's me or not." Gilbert glared at the man. "You look like one of them fancy lawyer types. That what you are?"

"My name is Daniel Hunter and yes, I am an attorney." The man stepped toward Gilbert and he took a hasty step back. "I have a restraining order here. Well, two of them. I'm serving you."

Gilbert put his hands behind his back when the two dark envelopes were thrust at him. "I ain't takin them. Who you trying to keep me from and why come? I ain't done nothing to anyone." At least he thought not where anyone would have seen him.

"The first is Kasey Marie York. The second is Suzan York, sister of Leah and Jason York, aunt to Kas—"

"I know who the fuck they be. I'm related to them people, why they thinking of keeping me away? I ain't gonna have no piece of paper tell me that I can't see my own kin." Especially not now, not when they'd done this to him. "'Sides, who's gonna know you gave me them papers anyways? There ain't no one here but the two of us."

The man nodded and Gilbert heard a sound behind him. He turned slowly to see three very large, very muscled men standing there. One of them had a camera or something pointed right at them.

"This is my friend Jared Stone and his foreman Thomas Conley. The one holding the camera is Royce, my brother. He is the one I'd be afraid of if I were you." Daniel grinned. "He wants you to be pissy about this and try to…what did you call it, Royce?"

"Try to fuck with Kasey again. She and I have come to an understanding. I understand that you're a fucking piece of shit and she understands that if you come near her again, I'm going to." At this point, the man shrugged. "I'm going to fuck you up. Badly."

Gilbert thought it was the grin that terrified him the most. The man looked like he'd gladly tear his throat out and then piss in the open sore and he'd said it with a calmness and a very matter of fact way that Gilbert had no doubt that he'd do just what he said he would. Gilbert took another step back and hit the wall behind him. The envelopes were shoved in his hands as he worried about whether or not he was going to

173

piss himself or not. Before he could get a grip on his bladder and his terror, Royce stepped forward.

"Here." Something else was shoved in his hands. "There's ten grand there. If I were you, I'd leave town. Tonight. And I'd never look back. Trust me when I tell you, you'll live much longer if you don't."

"You can't go threatening a man. 'Specially if'n it's being taped." At least Gilbert thought you couldn't. When Royce stepped closer, Gilbert pissed himself.

"Stay away from my wife. If I even hear that you breathed in her direction, I will hunt you down, cut you to pieces, and throw your worthless piece of shit hide all over the ground and let the rats eat what's left."

Gilbert heard some movements and it was then that he realized that at some point, he'd closed his eyes. Opening them one at a time slowly, he saw that he was alone in the hall. Still holding the envelopes and the cash in his hands, he tried five times to get his key in the lock before he got inside.

Throwing anything he could wrap his hands around in the trash can in his room, Gilbert was out the door again and heading down the stairs less than five minutes after he had his "close encounter." Flagging down the first taxi he saw, he was heading toward anywhere he could before looking down at the money.

There was a lot of it too. Mostly twenties, but there were a lot of fifties and a few hundreds as well. He straightened it all up and put it in various places on his person. He being a thief made him know where to hide money when it was necessary. By the time the taxi pulled in front of the airport, Gilbert had convinced himself that Royce had offered him a vacation and that it was going to be all paid by him. He was back to his old self again by the time he made it up to the counter.

"Jamaica. I need to get me some time in the sun and quit this here place." He paid for his ticket and was pleased to see he'd have lots to play on. He had a second or two of thinking that he'd hit his good buddy Royce up for some more if'n he needed it, but dismissed that idea right away. "Don't wanna wear out the welcome rug, not with him a marryin' my daughter. Nope, I think I'll find myself a good job and live the high life."

Gilbert was settled on the plane before he remembered his wet pants. *Hell,* he thought, *I'll buy me some new ones when I get meself settled.* Gilbert was going to be a happy man, he thought about himself.

~~~

Daniel had watched the man leave the cheap hotel. He was sitting in his car with his friends when his cell phone went off. He smiled when he saw who it was.

"Hello, sweetheart. What's going on?" Kasey snorted. "You really should try and stop that before the baby comes. What'll you say to him if you hear him do that?"

"I'll say that it's the easiest way to convey that the person you're talking to knows you think he is full of shit. What have you done, Daniel Anthony Hunter? And do not tell me nothing. I'm a lot smarter than you think I am and apparently, you think I'm fairly stupid."

He knew that someone had told her about her father. Royce was going to kill him for this because he'd promised his brother that she'd never find out. He tried to think of something that would get him in the least amount of trouble.

"I thought it was the best way to keep you safe. I didn't want anything to happen to you and my nephew." Silence. "Kasey? Are you mad at me?"

Still nothing, but he could hear voices in the background and then those too were muffled. When she came back on the line, he closed his eyes against the sudden headache he could feel coming on.

"Yes," she said with laughter. "Yes, furious. Now tell me what you did so that I can get over it and we can move on. And if you don't tell me right now, I'm going to figure it out, be pissed at you more, and it will hurt our relationship from now on. So, just spill it."

Daniel spilled it. Even his brother's part in it. She didn't ask many questions, but she did tisk at him several times. By the time he was finished he had watched her father go to the airport and buy a ticket. He was about ready to board the plane when she spoke.

"Where are you now?" He told her. "I see. And Royce, is he with you? Or is he making sure he's on the plane and not just pretending?"

"He had a meeting at the office. I volunteered to watch and make sure." He swallowed hard. "Are you really pissed off?"

She didn't say anything for several seconds. It seemed an eternity, but it really was only seconds. He'd watched his watch to be sure.

"I should be, you know." He didn't let go of the breath he was holding. "I should be with both of you. But I can't be. I know...he would have come and come again until one or all of you would have killed him."

He knew that was what Royce had said he'd do. Daniel wanted to believe that his brother wouldn't kill anyone, but he'd seen the look in his eye when he'd talked about Kasey. Getting out of his car, he walked to the gates and watched the planes take off. His friend at the counter gave him the flight number and a short nod.

"He's gone. And I don't expect him to return. Not for a long while anyway." Daniel nodded at Jared and Conley and they started back toward town with Jared driving much too fast. "I'll be at the office later if you want to talk."

"Oh you can bet on that. But first, I have to hunt down my maybe future husband and give him a hard time about this." Her laughter made him feel a little better. "Daniel?"

"Yes, love." He was smiling then, feeling like he'd conquered the whole world. "What is it?"

"You do anything like this again, ever, and I will find you, cut your nuts off to your dick, and serve it to you with vegetables." Then the line went dead.

Daniel put his phone on the seat beside him and took several deep breaths. Christ almighty, that was scarier than anything he'd ever heard before. He knew it was something that she'd try her best to carry out and thought that was what scared him the most.

CHAPTER 20

The trial. That's all he could think about was *the trial*. He was being sued by not only the Hunter Corporation, a place he'd given years of his life too, but by seven woman that he couldn't even begin to remember. Mike looked over at the paper again, the one that named all the females he'd supposedly abused and treated badly while in his employment. May Simpson.

She claimed that he had kept her from being promoted three times and had made her have sex with him in the locker room on several occasions. He'd had sex with every one of the women who had worked for him so that didn't really narrow it down. Well, not all, he remembered suddenly. That bitch Kasey hadn't. But this May person was saying that he'd forced her.

Mike had never "forced" anyone in his life. At least not after he'd gotten them where he'd wanted them. Grinning, he thought about that and then frowned.

That wouldn't be considered force. No way. Yes, he did dangle some prize in front of them. A promotion, maybe some extra pay, but they should have known that he had no way of giving them that. It was their own stupidity that had gotten them there, not him forcing them.

He looked at the next name on the list of women. Gertrude Best. He vaguely remembered her. She'd been a pretty little thing. Just graduated from college somewhere and needed a job while she did some shit or another that would get her into someplace he didn't give two shits about. She'd hurt him if he had the right girl. Punched him in the nose when he'd made love to her. She'd screamed something about rape for awhile until…he couldn't rightly remember what had shut her up, but she'd not bothered him again.

The rest of the names meant just as little to him. There was one name on the list, the one that kept pounding at him every time he saw it. Kasey M. York, the girl form when he'd been fired.

He'd felt his blood pressure rise whenever she was mentioned or he thought about her. The fucking cunt had told them, his boss, some lies and now he had no job, no way of getting on, and now he was marked as well. He looked down at the bracelet on his ankle and cursed it again.

He couldn't go twenty-five feet beyond his domicile, the judge, then that brother of Hunter's, had told him—several times—not with that fucking lock on his leg. What fucking bullshit was that, he wanted to know? He couldn't go to the bar down the street, couldn't go to the corner drug store; hell, he couldn't even go to the fucking mailbox without calling some prick and telling him where he was going. He did it too. He hated the way they'd made him feel when he'd not done it the one other time.

He'd been out there with his bills in his hand—another thing he was fucking pissed about, not having money to pay anything—and talking shit with his good friend that had just moved in next door…Benny something. The police had come around the corner like the place was a bank being robbed. Three cruisers pulled up in front of where he was standing with their guns pointed at him before he could even take a breath.

"Put your hands up and drop to your knees, now," one of them shouted in his and Benny's direction. "Now."

Mike looked over at Benny, wondering what the hell he'd done, when one of the cops shot a bullet at them. Both him and Benny dropped right fucking down after that. When the police started up to the walkway, still all ready to drop someone, he glanced over at his buddy again and was surprised to see one of them cops helping him up off the ground. Before he could think he was going to be helped up too, he was being tackled like a common criminal.

"What the fuck are you doing, you stupid cock sucker?" He knew as soon as the cop on his back growled at him, he'd made a tactical error. Didn't shut him up, but he knew that it should have. "Get the fuck off me, you son-of-a-bitch, or I'm going to sue your fucking ass."

"You just try it, you stupid bastard, and let me show you how many bones I can break in your face before someone pulls me off you." Mike had never been overly bright, he would admit that, but there was no reason for this guy to speak to him that way. Before he could make another, no doubt ignorant comment, there was a voice that he'd recognized from numerous phone conversations.

"I would shut up now if I were you, Mr. White. These guys aren't your normal run of the mill officers. They work for me. Well, my brother, but they take orders from me."

Curtis crouched down so that Mike could see him now. He had a thought that he'd never seen the guy in jeans before and thought stupidly that he looked as good in them as he did in a business suit. Mike started to say something, he wasn't sure what, when Curtis simply said, "quiet."

Suddenly, he was sitting up and the cops had moved away. Mike didn't try to stand, somehow knowing that he'd be right back where he was in seconds, but he did lean back, trying to make like it was okay for him to sit in the dirt with his fucking mail lying all over his lap.

"What the hell do you want? I haven't gone near your precious building," he said to him. "I've been nowhere, if you want to know that truth. I'm sort of tethered here."

Curtis laughed. "Yes, you are. And you're damned lucky you can move about at all. If I had my way, you'd be in prison awaiting trial, not living out among humans as if you're one of them."

"Hey. That's not right. You can't talk to me like—" The hand across his face made his head snap back so hard that he heard his neck pop. He closed his mouth with a snap.

"You will shut the fuck up and listen to me. You'll have this same treatment every time you so much as walk out the door beyond the twenty-five feet we had to give you. I don't like you very much, White, and I hope that for your sake when you go to trial, you get a fucking fantastic lawyer because I'm going for the max on this." Curtis stood up. "If I were you, I'd enjoy what I could of the outside world because when I'm through with you, you'll never see the light of day again."

That had been two weeks ago. And now here he was, the night before the trial. The police had been outside his apartment since the jury had been selected and he'd been with his dumb fuck lawyer once since then. He just knew that he was completely fucked.

The guy that had been assigned to him was Wilbert Fulton. What kind of person didn't change their name so that they'd have to go their entire life called Wilbert was beyond him. He was scheduled to come and take off the bracelet and take him to court within the next hour. At least that was the plan he'd been told yesterday. Mike thought about his own plan.

He was going to get the hell out of here as soon as the stupid thing was off and he didn't care how he did it or who he had to kill to make it happen. The gun Benny had given him last week was tucked right in the chair where he was sitting and the sucker was loaded too.

The knock at the door startled him. Wilbert was early, but it didn't matter. Mike had been prepared for that too. He'd been ready to go since yesterday morning. His bag was packed, he had all the cash he could get to under the circumstances, and he had his shoes on. He wasn't entirely sure they had to come off to take the fucking beeper off, but he was ready for that too with an extra pair of shoes in his bag. Getting a hard-on thinking about how this was going to make him a free man, Mike adjusted his cock as he walked to the door. It slammed open before he could get to it.

"Hello fuck-tard." Suddenly, Mike found himself on the floor and a knee at his back. "We are taking precautions, so you lay here real quiet like and you won't get hurt."

"No," he managed to squeak out before his arms felt as if they were being torn from the sockets. "You can't...let me up and let me sit in the chair. There isn't...what the fuck are you doing this for?"

"Chair, huh? Richey, go and check out what the little prick has hidden in the chair for us." The man at his back jerked his head around by his hair to look at him. "He'd better not find a nine millimeter there waiting for us."

Mike froze. That was exactly what was there. Looking around with his eyes because he couldn't move his head without becoming a bald man, he could see Benny standing near his chair with gloves on searching for the gun. Mike knew he'd been had when he also noticed that his good friend Benny Richey had a flack vest on that had the word POLICE written across it in bold white letters.

"You fucking cock-sucking son of a bastard. You're a cop." Mike's head hit the floor hard enough that he saw stars. "I'm suing you if you do that again."

And of course, the man at his back popped his head again. "This is not good, Mikey boy. Not good at all. Whatever will the judge think when he finds you've had a little piss shooter waiting on us? And one that didn't work too. Shame on you. Shame, shame."

Mike looked over at Benny again and glared. The bastard had sold him out and given him a gun that wouldn't work. Life couldn't be this cruel to him. He'd been a good person. Well, for the most part anyway. And now one stupid bitch tells lies and here was being treated like a criminal.

He was jerked up off the floor quickly. He wisely kept him mouth shut. Before he could get his bearings he was out the door and into a dark SUV and speeding down the road. Mike looked over at Wilbert when he laughed.

"Didn't you know a man in as much trouble as you shouldn't trust anyone? You're a very stupid man, very. And possession of a fire arm." Wilbert tisked at him. "Can't make you look like the outstanding citizen you seem to think you are."

"I'm going to get off this. And you know it if you read what I told you. I didn't do a damned thing to those women that they didn't beg for. Women like these are just begging for some time in the limelight."

Wilbert laughed again. "If you say so. I will defend you to the best of my ability because the courts say I must, but I hope you rot in a prison."

Mike had a thought that he might be fucked here, but they were pulling up in the back of the courthouse and he was again being jerked about. His lawyer was being treated like he was royalty while he was being tossed about like he was somebody's bitch. Things were going to change when he got out of this.

He was shoved in a cell and told to behave. Like he could do anything else. His hands were cuffed behind him and there was a bar between his ankles that kept him from walking correctly. He was handed an orange vest that had been pulled over his head before he'd left the house, but it wasn't until just now that he realized that it was a flack vest. He frowned when he thought about why someone would think he needed it.

He looked up when the door finally opened and three police officers he'd never seen before came in. He was suddenly nervous, terrified, and sick all at once. One of them barked at him that if he had to go, now was the time to do it. Go where he couldn't think, unless they were letting him go because they'd figured out it was all a lie, but the officer nodded to the single toilet in the corner. Glancing at it Mike shook his head no. There was no way he was pissing in front of these guys. He just knew they had no intentions of letting him have a moment.

~~~

Royce looked up when Mike White was brought into the room. He grinned when Mike staggered a couple of steps, but moved to his seat next to his lawyer after that. Royce was very happy to see that the prick was afraid of him.

"Behave or I'll send you home." He looked over at Kasey when she spoke. "I mean it. You behave or I'll make your brothers take you home and lock you in the closet until this is over."

He snorted, a nice little habit he'd picked up from Kasey. She raised her pretty brow at him, something he was sure she'd picked up from him, and nodded. He felt rather than heard someone move behind him.

"I wouldn't if I were you." He did glance behind him and saw Jared Stone standing there. "Jared, you know I'll kick your ass if you touch me right now. And that pretty little wife of yours will be working that new site all on her own for a little while."

"Then don't make me have to kick your ass. Besides, she brought in the big guns. My mom and dad are both here." Royce looked over at the Stones and nodded while Jared laughed. "My mom said to tell you that as far as she's concerned, she and your mom can bring you to heel in no time."

Royce thought he was right. Mrs. Stone terrified him as much as his own mother did. He'd never tell her that, but he was reasonably sure she knew it already. Jared sat down next to him and stretched out his long legs.

"You're so going to pay for this, you know that, right?" Jared grinned and nodded. Royce leaned closer to Kasey and whispered in her ear. "And you are as well. Keep it up, love, and your bottom will be nicely pinked up when you go to the doctor tomorrow."

Royce rubbed his hand over her belly. She was nearly due now and he was getting more and more excited every day. They were married now, had been for about five months, and they were having a blast. And as soon as their son was born, they were going to have their honeymoon. He wasn't even considering this trial an issue for them. She put her hand over his, moved it around her swollen belly, and he felt his son kick.

"He thinks you're full of shit too. Now I mean it. Behave yourself or I'll go into labor right now and you'll not get to see this bastard squirm."

He moved back in his seat, but didn't move his hand from the baby. He really was putting up a ruckus there and he loved to watch her belly move with his antics. He couldn't wait to hold him in his hands, cuddle him close. When the judge came in, they all stood up. Kasey moved a bit slower, but no one seemed to mind.

The special duty cop that they'd had watching over White stood up and told the judge how they'd gone by to pick up Mr. White and he'd ambushed them with a gun. White had stood screaming that it was a lie, that he'd never gotten the chance to get to his gun before they burst in on him, but the judge told him to shut up.

White apparently didn't know that shutting up meant not saying anything else and the judge finally told him that he'd put tape over his mouth if he said one more word.

"My courtroom is no place for you to be ignorant as well as a moron. And before you open your mouth again, know that I could put you away for more than your miserable life expectance if you say one more word." When White sat down again without saying anything, Judge Delaney said they'd have a separate trial for possession of the fire arm after this one. After that, they all settled down for what Royce thought was going to be very entertaining.

Opening statements were said and the trial began. Royce settled back to listen and as much as he wanted to laugh a few times, he did behave himself.

CHAPTER 21

Kasey remembered Elizabeth Black. When she was sitting up there on the witness stand Kasey remembered everything about her. She'd been called plaintive number four on the list of women.

Beth had been working there for six months when she'd simply quit. Kasey hadn't known why until this whole thing had started. She wondered about a lot of the others too and had been able to give Curtis all the names of the other women when he'd asked her. White had cornered Beth twice before she'd come to Kasey.

"He's making advances that make me feel creepy." Kasey had never been sure why the girl had come to her, but did try to help. "And he keeps touching me inappropriately."

Kasey pointed to the gun on the other girl's hip. "You could always use that on him. I don't mean shoot him," she hastily pointed out when the girl looked ready to explode. "I just mean hit him with it. That should tell him you're not interested quicker than just saying it."

"But I really need this job. There're not a lot of places that will hire a female guard, especially one that carries a gun. They think we're going to go all PMS on them. Not that it's not tempting sometimes, but I'd never do that."

189

Kasey had to hide a smile at the PMS comment and moved on quickly. "You could just go to HR. Human Resources have those posters up all over the break room telling you how to contact them and how no one would know about it."

Beth nodded then shook her head. "He'd find out, I just know it. And then it will be all over for me."

Kasey was pretty sure she was right. It was the reason she'd never gone to HR about White. They'd talked for a little while longer and then it seemed to be the end of it. Until a few weeks later when Beth simply wasn't at work anymore. At the time, she thought the girl had had enough and was happy for her. But listening to her tell her tale made Kasey feel like she'd let the girl down somehow. Kasey brushed at some tears just as Royce took her hand.

"You don't have to be here, honey. They would understand if you didn't come here until it was your turn. This can't be good for you or the baby." He nipped at her earlobe as he continued. "I could go home with you and we could take another nap. That seemed to relax you a lot last night."

She flushed all over thinking how he'd relaxed her through several climaxes and right into a coma. She looked at him and he growled low, and she nearly told him to get moving. Christ, nine months pregnant and she was like a nymphomaniac where this man was concerned.

She'd been tense all day. The trial was moving along at a good pace, but she knew her turn was going to come up soon. She'd told everyone at dinner that she was tired and needed to lay down. She was coming out of the bathroom in their room when she saw Royce come through the door.

"I thought I'd give you a back rub or massage your feet for you. Maybe you will sleep better that way." She still marveled at the fact that he was her husband and that he liked touching her. "Besides, the baby might like to hear about his daddy's day."

They'd been told the week before that sex was no longer an option. She had lost her mucus plug earlier in the week and the doctor had told them she was getting closer. The Braxton Hick contractions were getting stronger and it was just a matter of time now.

She'd lain down on the bed with him and he started rubbing her shoulders then her spine and finally, he was at her butt. He was rolling her to her side more when he brushed against her full breast.

"Roll to your back. I want to touch you." She did that without much thought and moaned when he tweaked her nipple. "Your breasts are so large right now. Full and so responsive."

Before she could say anything to him, he leaned down, took her nipple into his mouth, and suckled it through her gown. She arched her back, wanting him to take more, and felt her panties soak. She moved her legs to try and alleviate some of the pressure building there when he moved them open for him.

"Royce, we can't," she started. "The doctor said that we—"

"He said no sex. I'm going to give you pleasure. Just lay back, sweetheart, and let me have some fun. I promise you that you'll feel much better when I'm through."

While he took her nipple again, he settled between her legs. She closed her eyes, feeling overwhelmed and needy when she felt him slide his fingers under her panties.

"Christ, you're wet. And fucking hot. I don't want you to hold back, baby. When you want to come, let go." Royce moved his fingers into her and pressed her clit hard. "Come, Kasey, come for me."

The climax was soft and moved over her slowly. She had had a few like that in the last few months. While they did satisfy her some, they didn't last long. She started to roll to her side to sleep when she felt his mouth over her mound.

"Royce," she cried out when he sucked hard on her clit. His fingers moved in and out of her quickly now and his mouth didn't stop nipping. Before she could stop herself she had one hand wrapped tightly in his hair the other cupped her tender breast.

"That's it, baby. Make them ache." He moved his mouth along her inner thigh then nipped there. "Come again for me, Kasey. Come hard so that I can taste your sweetness."

She came twice more. Once when he'd commanded her to and the next time when he got up on his knees and undid his pants. His cock was hard and dark with need. She wanted to touch him, to take him into her mouth, but he fisted himself and came hard all over her, saying her name over and over as he did. She'd slipped away after that and hadn't awakened until this morning.

She squirmed on her seat again. It was as if the seats in this place were made to make a person feel like every bone in their body was crunching together. She glanced over at White and wondered how he could be so calm and relaxed-looking. She started to ask Royce when another person was called to the stand. A Gertrude Best, a name she'd not heard in years.

Gurt had been there at the beginning. She and Kasey had been hired in around the same time, Kasey about a week before the girl started. Kasey was amazed at how much the woman had changed and it wasn't until she took the stand that Kasey figured out just how much.

192

"Miss Best, could you tell us in your own words what happened the day you had a private meeting with Mr. White?" Curtis said to her gently. "There's no rush."

"He raped me." The words came out slowly as a wand was put at her throat. The sound was tinny and monotone. "He hit me with a bat and then he raped me."

Curtis nodded and handed her a box of tissues. "Is that how you came to have your throat injured? From the bat when he'd hit you?"

"No. Later. When I told him I would go to police." The girl wiped at the tears with her tissue. "He came to my house. He came with a gun."

Kasey felt the baby stir. Not like he'd done before, but a tightening around her middle that hurt almost. She rubbed her hand over him and tried to soothe him as Gurt continued to speak.

"He said I was to be still. Quiet. Told me to stop talking to others. I said no. I didn't see the gun until too late."

"What happened next, Miss Best? Tell us what he did next." Curtis' voice was soft, lulling almost. She looked over at him as she felt another pain, this one harder.

"Said he'd shut me up. Then he pulled out the gun. It was at my head and I fought him. I thought he was going to kill me. He…noise was loud and he laughed. Said how he had shut me up for good."

White jumped up from his seat screaming at them. Kasey didn't know what was being said because she was hurting badly now. She reached for Royce's hand and he turned to look at her as another pain grabbed her. She looked at his mouth moving, but couldn't hear anything coming out. Suddenly, Willow, her new friend, was standing next to her. Then nothing.

~~~

Royce watched them prep her. He'd been told that he needed to leave several times now, but he wasn't budging. He held her hand the entire time they talked gently to his wife.

He tried not to think about her slipping from her chair in the court room. That alone had aged him fifty years or so. But the blood had made him feel faint until one of his brothers, he thought it was Jesse, had shoved him away so that someone could have a look at her.

"She's in labor. Hard labor if I don't miss my guess. Your Mrs. here is going to have a baby soon. Here if we don't get her going." The man had introduced himself twice to Royce, but all he could wrap his mind around was that Kasey was in labor.

The ride to the hospital was made slowly, very slowly if he was asked about it. And as soon as the ambulance came to a sudden stop the doors flew open, and she was being jerked out with a cry.

"The attendant isn't suing you," Jesse had told him earlier. "Not because you offered to pay him not to, but because he said he should have known that you'd be scared when she was being brought in. He said to tell you that you have a hell of a left hook."

Royce flushed when his mother snorted at them. "I should have beaten you more as a child is what I'm thinking. What will you do when your own son hits someone without provocation?"

"He made her cry. Was I supposed to just stand by and let them make her cry?" She snorted again, a sound he was beginning to hate more and more daily. "And I didn't really mean to hit him. She cried out and I hit. It was a reflex."

His mom didn't say anything more, but he could tell she wasn't all that thrilled with him still. When Kasey said something to the nurse and she laughed Royce took her hand again.

"You do know that you're making their job harder, don't you? Or do you even care?" He didn't say anything to her question because frankly, he didn't. "Why don't you go and tell your family what's happening? The doctor said I had about an hour yet. But that everything was going just fine."

"I'm not leaving you. The way you seem to be running though this, I'll step out the door and my son will be in first grade before I get back. I'm staying." He glared at the nurse when she huffed at him. "I want to be here for you. I can't be here if everyone keeps sending me—"

The grip on his hand nearly had him cry out himself. Royce heard the beeping on the monitor go berserk as her fingers began to dig deep into his hand. He stepped into her view and told her to breathe with him. She glared but seemed to relax as the monitor slowed again. He vaguely heard a door open then close behind him before he heard the booming voice of the doctor behind him.

"Well, young lady, I see you waited for me to show up. Let's get you examined and see how much longer—" The monitor started screaming again and it was all Royce could do not to ask Kasey to let up. "Well, well, I guess we're a little more progressed than when you came in. Let's have a look, shall we? Royce, you want to—" He glared at the doctor who simply laughed. "I just wanted to see that look. You have my nurses thinking you might commit some sort of fiery dance on them if they cross you. Might want to practice that one for later if you have a daughter. Might keep her safe from boys like you when she gets to dating."

Royce just wanted to get through this one, thanks. He held Kasey's hand while the doctor had her put her feet up in the stirrups. She mumbled about it hurting and that she wanted to push when the doctor asked her.

Push? Royce tried to remember when that happened in the books he'd been studying up on and realized that was the end. He started to protest about things suddenly going really too fast when the monitor went off again.

"I think we should think about this. Things are—"

"All right, young man, get yourself ready. We're about to have us a baby. Kasey, love, when you feel the urge to push, you go right on ahead. And remember what the people in those classes told you, go at it like you have to take a large crap." Royce had no more time. He was about to have a baby and he realized suddenly he wasn't sure he was ready.

They laid little Royce Lee York Hunter on his mother's chest eighteen minutes and forty-one seconds later. Royce knew because he'd had the misfortune of hearing the nurse tell everyone that time frame seventeen times as they worked on his wife. Lee, as they were going to call their son, started rooting around as he felt his mother's skin next to his mouth.

"Got yourself a hungry little man there, Mr. Hunter. He wants his dinner right now, not even five minutes old." The nurse helped Kasey pull her gown down and bare her breast. "Go ahead and try to nurse him, Mrs. Hunter. It will do you both a world of good."

Lee latched onto her nipple like he'd been doing it forever. Royce smiled. He supposed he had been. Watching his son nurse was perhaps the best thing he'd ever seen in his life.

"He's doing it. He's really doing it. Oh, Royce, I want hundreds more just like him." The doctor laughed and they both ignored him. Royce reached down and ran his finger over the baby's tiny little head.

He was beautiful. Perfectly formed and pink. The nurse told him that his first reading was perfect and she expected no less of him when they did the second one. When they asked to take him to be cleaned up, Kasey watched with tears in her eyes as they took him away. Royce followed them to the little basinet in the corner.

"He weights seven pounds and ten ounces and is eighteen and three quarters inches long." Royce pulled out his phone, snapped a picture of his baby, and put in the information as the nurse gave it to him. He wasn't sure why anyone but he and Kasey would care what size his head or chest was, but he typed it in all the same. When she told him that he was perfect, as he'd already guessed he was, he put that in there as well and sent it to his family, including his newly acquired one with Jay and Suzy. He put his phone away and walked back to Kasey.

"I love you. Thank you for my son. He's perfect." He kissed her again and reached into his pocket and pulled out the blue box he'd been carrying around for three weeks. "I know that you don't care for jewelry that much, but I thought you'd like this."

He'd had it custom made for her. And when she opened it and she cried, he was sure he'd made the right choice. It had taken a lot of figuring and a great deal of help from her uncle Jay.

The bracelet was filled with small charms and pictures. There was a blue bootie that he'd had made with the baby's initials on it and the year. A pair of rings like the ones they wore with their initials and the year they'd gotten married. The pictures were in small frames and that was what had taken the most time to get together.

Several of them were of them together. There was one each of them as a baby. Jay had found a whole box of pictures when he'd gone to clean out his sister's apartment. He'd wanted to put all of them on there for her, but there were hundreds of them and he was sure she'd not be able to lift her arm with them there.

But the ones that he'd taken the most care with were the ones of her mom. Two of them were of Leah alone, one of her while pregnant with Kasey. The other when she'd been on vacation somewhere before she'd been ill, Jay had told him. Then there were the ones of mother and daughter together.

Leah had been a beautiful pregnant woman. Her face glowed with happiness, much like Kasey's had. The other one was of Leah holding her daughter when Kasey had been around seventeen and had just graduated from high school. Jay had said that Kasey should have graduated the year before, but she'd thought herself in love with this boy and wanted to wait for him. Turned out he had only wanted her mind and not her heart.

"It's beautiful. Oh, Royce, it's so beautiful." She ran her fingers over the blue bootie and then looked up at him when the frame was blank. "For Lee, I guess?"

"Yes. I did have them put this one there." He showed her the one of the sonogram before he'd been born that showed he was a male. "But I wanted to get one of him, the one that I just took, put on there too."

She pulled him down for a kiss and everything was right in the world for him. They gave them Lee back while they waited in recovery. The nurse asked and was granted permission to go and get the families. The room filled quickly with women cooing over the baby and the men slapping him on the back.

Yes, Royce thought, life was perfect.

CHAPTER 22

The trial continued on without Royce and Kasey until the ninth day. The day she was going to tell her side of the story. She wasn't thrilled about her time away from her son, but since Annamarie was keeping him for them, she felt marginally better. She was sworn in and asked to say her name.

"Kasey Marie Hunter." The room erupted in laughter when she had to stutter over her name twice. "I've only been married a short while, Your Honor, and I don't have to say it often."

"Don't you worry about it, Mrs. Hunter. When you've been married awhile, you'll remember it right quick." He glared at White when he snickered. "You'd best be on your best behavior. I've had about all I can take from you this week."

Kasey had heard how White had jumped from his seat to try and get to one of the other women who'd come to tell what had happened. A swift wrap on the head from the judge's gavel had stopped his forward motion enough that the bailiff was able to get him into cuffs and out of the room. Connie McIntosh had finished her horrific tale to just the judge and the jury and Curtis as the judge had thrown everyone else out. White had been pissed to find out that she'd had a baby by him.

But the DNA had come back positive, well, ninety-nine point seven percent positive. White, it seemed, had taken exception to the other point three percent. He said that the test had been rigged.

"She can't be here. It's a conflict of interest or something like that. She's got the family tied up all in a neat bow to try and frame me," White shouted. His lawyer had been "fired" three days before. "I don't think she should be allowed to try and take me down with her being married to the man who is accusing me."

The judge hit his gavel on the desk and made her jump. He apologized to her and looked over at Curtis. Both men were grinning. "Counselor, do you have any objection to me changing this proceeding right now?" Kasey wasn't sure, but she thought that they'd hoped this would happen. "I don't want the Hunter Corporation to come under fire for this. What do you say we change things up a bit?"

"I'm all for it, Your Honor. I would like to be a part of this if Mr. White doesn't mind. I would really hate to be simply dismissed out of turn." They both turned to White and the judge asked him if he cared.

"If it means that I won't be tried by the Hunters, then okay. I guess. Would it mean that Shelia here doesn't get to say her part to anyone?"

"Nope, Shelia can't say a word against you. Not now, not ever." When Kasey started to say she wasn't Shelia, she saw Curtis shake his head slightly. He continued speaking to White. "Shelia will agree to whatever is necessary to get this moving in the right direction."

"Well then let's have at it. I would like to get myself home soon. Not that you all haven't been really accommodating, but I have to find myself a job and all. Bills to pay, you know." White nodded again as he continued. "Yeah, the faster we do this, the better I'd like it."

Kasey noticed that when a folder was brought to the judge and Curtis was given a copy that White sat up in his chair straighter. He kept looking at her and grinning like a fool, but she simply sat there. When she'd tried to move back to her seat, she was told to wait. So wait she'd done.

"All right then, Mrs. Hunter, continue with your side of the story." She looked at Curtis, who nodded at her when the judge had given her permission. Before she could speak, White jumped up.

"Now wait a damned minute. You said she couldn't tell her side of the story. You said that you were going to make this go better for me. I don't think Sally here is going to tell you anything different now than she'd been about to tell you."

"Her name isn't Shelia or Sally, you moronic idiot. Her name is Kasey. Kasey Marie York Hunter, the woman who is going to put you away for a very long time." Curtis tried to continue speaking over White, but he just wouldn't shut up. The judge finally had the bailiff draw his gun and point it at the man.

"You have got to be the dumbest man I've ever had the displeasure of meeting. What on earth made you think that I was going to do anything but try you and then sentence you?" When White started to speak again, the judge grinned. "I'd do what that man tells you. He retires in a few weeks and he's just itching to take out someone before he goes."

Kasey laughed. She couldn't help it. It was wonderful to see White get what he deserved. She looked at the judge. "Can I talk now?" He nodded at her. "I started working for the Hunter Corporation right out of high school. I was working my way through college at the time and it was a good paying job. Not a great job, but it paid well."

She looked over at Royce when he stepped through the door with their baby in his arms. He winked at her and sat right behind the table where Curtis had been sitting. She smiled then, the tension of telling this story going right out of her. She simply told it to him.

"I learned the job quickly and when things started to look like an opening would come up, I would apply. Every time I did, Mr. White would shoot me down. It was one thing or another, but ultimately, it came down to him telling me if I slept with him, he'd promote me without any problems."

"Did you?" Curtis asked from his position near the desk. "Did you sleep with Mr. White?"

She looked over at the man who had terrorized her for years. Who'd kept her from her mother sometimes and who on more than one occasion had hit her. She shook her head before answering. "No. He wasn't worth it. And I have much too much pride in myself to ever think that he'd be worthy enough to give me what he'd promised."

"There were other women. Others like you that he'd lied to. Did you know that he'd hurt them? That he'd made the same promises that he'd made you?"

She looked away from Royce, knowing that she'd made a mistake in not encouraging them to go to someone above White's head. "Yes. I'd had a few conversations with them. Not all of them, but a few. I...I, like them, believed that there wasn't anyone to help us. That we'd be lucky if we didn't lose our jobs or, worse yet, be black balled out of the kind of work we were good at." Kasey looked at the four women who had been there every time she'd been in the court room. "We were good at our jobs. Very good. What he did was...what White did to all of us was wrong. Not just because he'd raped and hit, but that we'd allowed it to happen to us. We should have been braver. Smarter even. I'm so sorry."

Gurt stood up and a hush came over the room when she did. "You saved me. He could have killed me that day, but I knew that I'd be letting you down if I died. You told me to kick his balls the next time he did anything to me. I tried. I lived because you told me that I was stronger than him."

May stood too and nodded. Then Shawna Parks. Kasey didn't know much about her other than she'd had a child before working there and had almost lost custody of her when White had told someone at the welfare office that she was a whore. Of course there was no evidence to say it, but her reputation had been blackened and she'd left town. She'd only been found when Kasey had remembered her father lived here still.

At the end of the day White was taken away and the jury was sent to deliberate all that they'd been told. Kasey went to her husband and new baby and cried all the way home. She wanted something from the Hunter Corporation and she wasn't sure how to get it. She called the only other person she knew who would understand her.

Bobbie met her at the office the next morning and the two of them started to work. By the third day of meeting, first there then at her home, the two women had a proposal to give to the board.

~~~

Annamarie knew when she saw Kasey that the woman was going to blow them out of the water. She had an air about her that said "fuck off." Annamarie thought maybe she'd put her new daughter-in-law on the next committee she had to form. The woman looked like she could hold her own.

"In the past several weeks I've noticed an expansion in the security department. I think that as a company Hunter Corporation should work at—"

"You're the Hunter Corporation now too, sweetheart. You own as much of the company as I do." Annamarie looked at Royce when he cut his wife off. "If you want to try something here then by all means, simply tell me what it is and I'll make it happen for you."

"No. I mean thanks, but no. I want to make you make this happen as you said, but not because I want it but because it's a sound idea. And unless you make the company move more to the twenty-first century then I'm not so sure I want any part of it."

Annamarie laughed when Royce and Daniel sputtered. She wasn't surprised when Jesse just leaned back in his chair. "Oh come now. You can't be upset with her for voicing her mind. I, for one, would like to hear how we've lagged behind. Go on, Kasey. Tell us what we can do."

"What is it then? Are we not hiring enough females? Do we not have enough female bathrooms? Come on. Tell us how we've gotten so antiquated." Curtis rubbed his forehead as he continued. "I'm sorry. I'm really sorry, Kase. Please, tell us."

"She thinks we should educate our employees. And not just the security team, but all of us. Had we been better equipped to handle someone coming to us, none of this would have gotten out of control." Jesse got up and took the folder from Kasey that she was using. "I've been looking at what you've put together. You're a smart cookie."

"Have you been going to Jesse and not me?" Royce sounded hurt. "Kasey, you know I would have helped you with anything."

"No, I didn't go to him." Kasey jerked her folder from Jesse. "And I may have to put him through the privacy classes twice. Where the hell did you learn about this?"

Jesse winked at her. "I'm learning how to observe and report. You know that nothing goes on around here that I'm not at least partly aware of. Besides, you had to log the computer time in. Shouldn't have looked on all those sites without checking to see whose computer you were using."

Annamarie looked at Bobbie when she said, "damn it," and then laughed when she glared at Jesse. "Remind me next time a girl calls in for you that I tell her your home phone number. Ungrateful child. You should be horsewhipped taking her thunder away like that." Bobbie smacked at him before she smiled at Kasey. "Go on, Kasey, tell them."

Nodding, she continued. "Those women should have been able to go to someone higher than White. I should have gone to someone, but who? There's no list that tells us who to go to. There isn't anyone that is there for us on our level, not HR or even a member of management. Most all of those women worked third shift, as did I. White could pretty much do what he wanted because there was no one on those shifts that we could talk to that had anything to do with him. I'm not saying that you need to hire someone that would be there on the off chance—"

"Yes, we do. I know just where you're going. A sort of neutral person. One that has no say in security but knows the people who work in it. A person that when the door is closed to their office, nine hundred people aren't aware that you've gone in here to speak your mind. Also the rumor mill won't be so bad with all sort of things going on before the first word is spoken because no one will be the wiser." Jesse started making notes as he continued. "The office would be on another floor than the one we have the security office on. The person we get needs to be aware of the laws governing HR and also know how to defuse a situation without it becoming a media playground. Oh, Royce," he said suddenly. "That office on the second floor, the one that we have the luncheons in. That would be perfect."

Kasey looked over at Annamarie when she lost control of the meeting. "I just wanted them to give me a phone number that they could set up weekly meeting and training classes with. I didn't mean for them to spend money like they had it to spare."

"You've saved them a great deal, honey. If we have the right people in place, then there won't be any more Whites in the building and no more lawsuits. This is just the breath of fresh air that they need." Annamarie looked at Bobby when she laughed.

"You probably saved them from killing White with this. This will give them something else to focus on besides whether or not he'll get off. The turd seems to think he will and he gives me the creeps the way he keeps looking around and licking his lips."

Annamarie had noticed him doing that too. Especially when Kasey was in the court room. She wondered if Royce had noticed and decided that he hadn't. If he had, or any of the boys for that matter, then White would already be dead. She looked up when Curtis called for Kasey.

Three hours and four large pizzas later they had a committee, a person to run the program they were piecing together, and Kasey Hunter was now an official board member. She still looked a little dazed about it all when they went to the office so that she could nurse little Lee. This time, she asked Royce if she could sit with her.

Lee was a beautiful baby. He had a full head of dark hair and his downy skin was so soft that Annamarie found herself touching him just to feel it beneath her fingers. She'd never been more in love with anyone as she was her first grandson.

"They really will do it, won't they?" She looked up at Kasey when she asked. "They really will just put me in charge of the whole thing like I have any idea what the hell...heck I'm doing."

"I'm sure you know a great deal more than you think. You banned them together easily enough." Kasey snorted. "Well, you certainly have my vote for pulling it off."

"You're just saying that because you want to watch Lee when I have to go to meetings." Annamarie nodded. "Okay, but you know all you have to do is ask. Other than me being his lunchbox, he pretty much doesn't care who holds him."

"Not true. I saw him cry his head off when that cook of yours held him. I don't think he liked him one bit." Of course, the man had been terrified out of his mind, but she didn't say that. Best to let that one go.

"I don't know. I just don't want to disappoint anyone."

Annamarie laughed gently and told the girl she couldn't even if she tried.

CHAPTER 23

The jury came back the next afternoon. Royce had wanted Kasey to stay home, but she said she needed to be there. He didn't want to be there so he thought her being beside him would be a tad easier. He held her hand and had his son in his arms. He was sure that White was going to be convicted, but on what charges he had no idea.

When everyone sat back down they looked over at the jury when the judge asked them if they'd reached a verdict. The foreman stood as asked and she started reading the charges.

Guilty. On all nine charges, he was guilty. Before the judge could say more, White stood up.

"You can't convict me, you stupid bitch. I didn't do a damned thing to those women that they didn't want." He turned to the judge. "You have to tell them to try again. You make them go back in that room until they come out with a better verdict. I'm not going to jail. There is no way I'm going to jail."

"Then what do you propose we do with you? Let you go? I don't think so. You have to pay for the crimes you've committed. And to do that you will serve—"

Royce would remember the next few seconds for the rest of his life. He would never…no, that's not right, he could not believe that someone could do so much damage so quickly and then take her own life.

Gertrude Best had been in the court room daily with them. She'd been quiet and reserved for the most part, only getting upset once or twice, but had delivered her story with as much dignity as anyone could under the circumstances. And every day she'd come in with her wand at her throat. Royce knew that she'd never been questioned about it after she'd been on the stand.

The little gun had gone off before the judge had had a chance to make a date for sentencing. Gurt had pointed the little wand at White on several occasions throughout the trial, that when she'd done it this time no one had thought a thing about it. At least Royce hadn't. The *pop-pop-pop* had sounded long seconds before anyone moved and the last pop had gone off before Gurt could be reached. The final bullet had torn through her chin and up through her brain in seconds.

While everyone rushed to the dead woman, no one moved to the man who lay bleeding to death on the floor. Gurt had been an excellent shot. She'd gotten White twice in the throat and once in the cheek. There was no saving him after they realized that he wasn't killed like they had assumed. Royce wondered after if anyone had really tried.

It had taken them four hours to get everyone's statements. Royce had tried several times to get Kasey to take Lee home and wait for him, but she'd stood next to him, at his side when the reports had come, and then again when they were all questioned. She was eerily quiet on the drive home.

"She had this planned for a long time, didn't she?" Kasey finally asked when they were in bed together. "She knew what she was doing the moment she'd come to the courthouse."

"Yes. I think she had a plan to kill White even before we'd approached her to tell her side of what had happened." Royce didn't tell anyone that he thought that Gurt had done them all a favor by killing White. He thought it, but didn't voice it. "She had had her little gun made when she'd still been in the recuperating stages after he'd shot her."

"I wish we could have talked more. I wish she could have… I was going to ask her to help me with the program. I thought she'd be an inspiration to everyone knowing that good things could come to you if you didn't think of yourself as a victim. I guess I was wrong."

He pulled her tight in his arms and kissed her shoulder. "You weren't wrong, love. You couldn't see how badly she'd been affected by what he'd done to her. I'm not sure anyone had."

She lay there for several minutes before she spoke again. "Royce, do you think the others will be all right? Do you think any of them are thinking about killing themselves?" She turned to him then. "Is there anything we can do for them?"

He nodded before he said anything. "We'll give them anything they need, baby. Anything. You work your magic on them and see what we can do to help them and we will. I swear if it is in my power to do it, they can have it."

He held her long after she'd gone to sleep and when Lee woke a few hours later, he went to the nursery to get him. He changed his diaper and took him to the big rocker just to hold him. Lee seemed to be all right with waiting on his food so Royce told him about his mom.

"You should see her went she gets all fired up about something. I'm telling you, son, it's a sight to behold. And boy, when she's…well, that's between mom and me. But she

211

can light me up pretty good too." Lee watched him as he spoke to him, never breaking eye contact. "You're going to be such a ladies man, kid. You just wait and see. But you won't be knocking any of them up before you say 'I do.' I did that and it turned out wonderful for me, but you can't expect to be so lucky. Here are words my brothers say all the time, 'don't tap it if you don't wrap it.' Words to live by."

"What a thing to say to a baby."

Royce looked up at Kasey standing in the doorway when she spoke.

"Are you seriously giving our ten day old son sexual advice?"

"You're never too young to be taught to respect the lady. Besides, you know you'll be giving any daughters that we have the same advice." She walked to him and started to kneel on the floor in front of the rocker. "Sit in my lap. I want to hold the two most important people in my life."

She slid into the chair and Royce handed her Lee. He cradled them both in his arms. He doubted there was a better feeling in the world than this.

"I have a news conference tomorrow with your mom. Your brother, I think, set it up a long time ago. Then we have a meeting with a reporter from the Daily Broadcast. Some guy by the name of Kyle Washington."

"Kylie Washington. It's a girl, woman. She and Jesse went to school together. She's a real ball buster. She was the one that got the last mayor impeached. She uncovered a ring of prostitution that he'd been running with campaign money." Royce stood when Kasey did. Lee had decided that he'd waited long enough.

He watched her nurse him. He was such a greedy little thing and he made noises that made Royce smile. Lee held his mother's finger while he ate his dinner.

"Annamarie said that he…Kylie has been on the story for some time and that she is the one who'd found two of the women for the trial. Do you think she knew about Gurt?" Royce told her that he didn't know. "I hope she didn't. I think that would be hard for her to live with if she did."

Royce hadn't had anything more to do with Gurt than to see her in the court room, and he was having a hard time with it. He could still see her blood on the wall behind her when she'd killed herself. "I guess we'll find out soon enough. She and Daniel meet on Monday morning. And from what I remember about her as a kid, she and Daniel didn't get along all that well. Seems she'd take exception to everything that he said.

~~~

Kylie Washington put down her phone and looked at her notes. She was really going to go to the Hunter building to see Daniel Hunter. She closed her eyes, trying to wipe out the hurt and pain that was there every time she'd thought about him. The pisser had made her mad every time she'd seen him when she'd been a teenager.

It had started in middle school, moved up through high school, and then into adulthood. Every time they saw one another, he would make her mad enough to make her want to kick him. But she'd remained the adult. And not only had she not put his nuts up around his eyes, she'd written a glowing article about him when he'd taken over the personal side of his brother's firm. Cushy job that it was.

She flushed then. She had walked into the same kind of job. Her daddy had owned the newspaper she worked for since before she was born. At least Royce had made himself into what he was; her dad had inherited it from his dad. She walked to her closet for the tenth time in the past three hours.

She didn't have a thing to wear to this. She wanted to look professional yet hardnosed. She wanted him to see that she could be feminine, yet still be a pro. She threw the last dress in her closet on the floor. Damn it, she wanted him to see that she'd turned into this drop dead gorgeous woman who had a few more brain cells then the normal women he dated. Fat chance.

By the time she cleaned up her bedroom and put the first thing she touched with her eyes closed into the bathroom to put on in the morning, she went to bed. Tomorrow, she was going to see the only man who had made her feel things she'd never felt before.

Kylie Washington had been in love with Daniel Hunter since she'd been ten years old.

ABOUT THE AUTHOR

I woke up one morning and decided to give play time to the people in my head who were keeping me awake. Little did I know that they would be so relentless and want their time right now! I wrote for the pure joy of it and to entertain my family and friends. But mostly it was to get more than an hour of sleep without a story playing out. Of course, the more I write, the more they want. So…well, as a result of sleepless days (I work through the night as a gun toting grandma – nope not a vigilantly but an armed security guard) I have lots of stories written.

Hello! My name is Kathi Barton and I'm an author. I have been married to my very best friend Sonny for at times seems several lifetimes – in a good way, honey. And together we have three wonderful children and then the ones we brought into the world - Paul and Dale Barton, Jason and Wendy Barton and Danielle and Ben Conklin. They have given us seven of the greatest treasures on Earth. They don't live at home seven days a week! No, seriously, seven grandchildren – Gavin, Spring, Ben, Trinity, Sarah, Kelly and Kian.

Follow Kathi on her blog:
http://kathisbartonauthor.blogspot.com/

Made in the USA
San Bernardino, CA
13 November 2013